READER PRAISE FO

"A real page turner"

"Love the Essien family"

"My new favourite author"

"Excellent"
"Great series"

"Fantastic"
"I want to be like Felix Essien when I grow up!"

ALSO BY KIRU TAYE

The Essien Series
Keeping Secrets
Making Scandal
Riding Rebel
Kola
A Very Essien Christmas
Freddie Entangled
Freddie Untangled

Bound Series
Bound to Fate
Bound to Ransom
Bound to Passion
Bound to Favor
Bound to Liberty

The Challenge Series
Valentine
Engaged
Worthy
Captive

Passion Shields Series
Scars
Secrets
Scores

Men of Valor Series
His Treasure
His Strength
His Princess

Others
Haunted
Outcast
Sacrifice
Black Soul

Keeping SECRETS

First Published in Great Britain in 2018 by
LOVE AFRICA PRESS
103 Reaver House, 12 East Street, Epsom KT17 1HX
www.loveafricapress.com

LOVE AFRICA
~~&~ PRESS ~~
African Love Stories

ISBN: 978-1-9164755-2-6
Also available as ebook and audiobook

To Elsie, you reminded me that ectopic pregnancy is a 21st century killer scourge in Nigeria. This story is dedicated to you, my best friend. May you continue to rest in peace until we meet again.

I miss you.

CHAPTER ONE

"MRS. ESSIEN, your husband is out of his coma."

Phone pressed against one ear, the other hand reaching for the remote control, Ebony bolted upright. Her hand shook as she fumbled to mute the television news channel she'd been watching. The discarded controller clanked onto the clear, glass-topped side table.

"D...did I hear you correctly? Felix is awake?" She couldn't hide the tremor in her voice, nor relax her tight-knuckled grip on the overstuffed arm of the upholstered cream sofa. Disbelief warred with hope, trampling all over her troubled mind.

"Yes, madam," the nurse said at the other end of the line.

Breath rushed out of her lungs. The living room turned blurry. She lowered her lashes and slumped backwards, the velvet cushions a haven of soft comfort. A tear seeped from the corner of her eye and rolled down her cheek. She didn't bother to wipe it. This didn't represent sadness. No. This spelt relief—pure and simple—at prayers answered. At last.

"Hello? Are you still there?"

Eyes flickering open, she took in the bare cream walls of the living room and her gaze landed on the pile of framed wedding photographs in the far corner, overshadowed by a dark wood sculpture of a couple cinched in passion.

Since she'd taken delivery of the photos, she hadn't been able to bring herself to put them up.

"I'm still here." She swiped another tear with the back of her hand and cleared her throat.

"How is he? When did he wake up?" The words rushed from her lips, relief now overtaken by excitement.

Soft laughter filtered through the phone. "Take it easy, madam."

Ebony grimaced. The respectful term for a woman only made her feel ancient; she'd prevented her household employees from using it to address her. But she didn't tell the nurse on the phone.

"Sorry," she said instead as she curled her lips with joy for the first time in weeks. She could forgive the woman who delivered such delightful news.

"No need to apologise. I understand, Madam," the nurse continued in a cheerful voice. "Your husband woke a few minutes ago. The doctor is with him now and he seems okay, considering his condition. There is a request on his note to contact you as soon as he wakes up. This is the reason for my call."

"Thank you so much, Nurse. I'll come to the hospital straight away." Ebony ended the call and sprang to her feet, ready to race to the bedroom to change.

Bad move. Her head swam, making her nauseated by the sudden movement, her stomach heaving like a turbulent sea.

Sinking back into the sofa, she breathed through the queasiness, head tilted slightly forward on her hands.

Oh, Lord. I hope I haven't picked up a stomach bug.

It'll teach her to buy street food. Last night, she'd craved *Kilishi* so much, she had to stop on the way home from hospital to pick up the beef jerky-style food cured and seeped in spices.

The omelette and toast she'd had for breakfast hadn't stayed down, to the dismay of the housekeeper. The poor girl had looked appalled at the notion she may have poisoned her mistress. Hence the reason Ebony had been sitting in the living room when her phone rang, instead of being already at the hospital, her usual routine.

Perhaps, the stress of the past few weeks finally caught up with her. Long days and even longer nights, staying up worried about Felix.

Her chin dipped into her chest and her shoulders slumped as a wave of guilt hit her.

I should've been there when he woke up. He should've seen me first. Not the nurse or doctor. Me, his wife. Today of all days, too. Is it fate that he woke on Valentine's Day?

"Aunty, are you okay?"

Ebony exhaled a sigh and lifted her head. The word 'aunty' gave her familial closeness to the addresser, a sense of not being alone in this mansion or dealing with faceless employees, but rather engaging with a member of the family.

Bisi, the housekeeper, stood beside her sofa twisting her hands, her anxiety plastered on her round face, her outfit— a blue check dress, white pinafore, and white sandals— creaseless and stainless, her hair plaited in neat straight cornrows, pulled into a bun at the back. The twenty-year old girl always took pride in her appearance. Living in meant Bisi became part of their household, which made her family.

Ebony curled her lips into a reassuring smile. "I'm more than okay. Stop worrying."

She stood carefully and this time, the world stayed the right way up.

"Just tell Kola that I'll be ready to go the hospital in thirty minutes."

"Yes, Aunty." The girl nodded. "I've packed the bag ready for you. Do you want me to skip class tonight, in case you need me?"

"No. There's no need for you to miss your lesson."

Ebony paid for Bisi to study Home Economics at their local college, with emphasis on Cookery after she discovered the girl's interest in food and flavours. She should tell her Felix woke up. But after waiting so long to get some good news, she wanted confirmation with her own two eyes before announcing it to the rest of the household staff.

"Thank you for packing the bag."

She patted the housekeeper on the shoulder and headed upstairs, bare feet slapping on cold marble. Crockery tinkled behind her as Bisi cleared up the teacup and saucer from the side table.

On the threshold of the master bedroom, she halted, taking in the space before her. The cream walls and dark wood effect reached here, too. The heavy mahogany frame of the massive bed and headboard has been specially ordered, the design bespoke. She remembered asking for the measurements for the mattress before she ordered luxurious Egyptian cotton sheets.

That had been before disaster struck. Neither one of them had slept in the bed since it arrived.

Blinking back tears, she crossed the floor, her toes curling into the velvety, beige shag-pile rug covering the hard slate.

She walked into the clothes closet and sucked in a sharp breath. Seeing the rows of Felix's shirts and suits always triggered unhappiness. Today, she should be jumping for joy. Yet, her chest tightened and the back of her throat hurt.

"This isn't how we planned it, Felix...." Her voice croaked.

She clutched his white shirt, inhaled deeply, and sobbed. Body racking, her legs gave way. She crumpled to the floor, the metal hook from the hanger clattering as it hit hard slate.

Could it be possible to feel intense joy and sadness all at the same time? One minute she wanted to sing her joy with a microphone. The next, she wished she could crawl into a cave a hide.

Worse, she couldn't shake the boulder of guilt weighing down her body. This was all her fault. She'd doomed her marriage right from the start. How else could she explain that she wore a wedding band, had a marriage certificate to boot, but had never felt the warm arms of her *husband* around her?

"Aunty, *Oga* Kola is ready for you." Bisi's voice sounded close.

Did I leave the bedroom door open?

10

Standing, Ebony took one last sniff of Felix's shirt before tossing it into the laundry basket. Though it had the crisp smell of detergent, it reminded her of the man before the accident.

"I'll be down in five," she said and entered the adjoining bathroom, keeping her face averted so the girl couldn't see her from the entrance. She listened to the receding footsteps as Bisi departed.

At the sink, she stared at her face in the mirror. Her exhaustion showed, twin dark shadows beneath eyes red from lack of sleep and crying.

Cool water from the tap calmed the puffy eyes. A couple of eye drops brightened the whites, and dabs of concealer hid her sullen skin. She applied some lip-gloss and brushed out her hair, letting the tresses hang loose. It helped to cover up her fatigue.

Just like she got good at covering up everything else. She couldn't reveal that all wasn't well in paradise.

She slipped on her shoes, grabbed her bag, and headed out to see her husband.

"Mr. Essien, you are in the Worthington Hospital in Lagos. You were in a car accident and suffered several injuries, including a head trauma, resulting in you falling into a coma," the doctor said after examining him thoroughly and offering him extra painkillers, which he rejected. He needed a clear head to chase away the fog lurking in his brain.

"How long have I been here?" he asked, anxiety coursing through him, prickling his skin.

"About six weeks. Can you remember what happened?" the doctor asked.

He'd barely taken in the physician's name, simply noting the man's position as a consultant surgeon in a reputable hospital and realising, from his looks, that they must be about the same age.

11

He racked his brain but couldn't remember anything about an accident.

And he couldn't shake the feeling of something being terribly wrong. Why couldn't he remember?

"No. What day is it?" he asked to get his bearing. The doctor told him. Stunned, a bolt of alarm shot down his spine. "And you say I've been in a coma for over a month?"

"Yes. What do you remember?" the doctor enquired again.

"The last thing I remember is being on my way to the airport with my driver."

Briefly, the doctor's face creased in a frown before he spoke. "There is no cause for alarm. Some memory loss is expected with the kind of head injury you suffered. You are a healthy young man and with time, I expect you to make a full recovery. In the meanwhile, we'll carry out some more tests and monitor your progress to ensure everything is healing as it should."

After the doctor left, he'd drifted back into a hazy, restless sleep.

He woke with a dull ache in his head. Before his eyes opened, he lifted his hand to his forehead, massaging it. Heavy, drooping lids blinked several times as his eyes adjusted to the bright sunlight coming through the window, the black and white motif print curtains pulled back and secured with sashes.

Raising his right hand, he flicked his wrist, expecting to see his gold watch. Instead, a plastic hospital tag with his name hung in its place. Adhesive tapes secured the IV cannula to his left hand. He didn't move it, so as not to dislodge the needle stuck into his veins. However, he'd insisted on having the catheter removed. About time he started using his legs again when nature called.

He scratched the stubble on his chin. Someone had been shaving him regularly. A nurse? Considering his room had the opulence of a hotel suite than that of a regular hospital ward, it could be part of the service. A quick brush over thick hairs on his head confirmed he needed a haircut, though.

He scanned his white-walled surroundings, where a TV screen hung on the wall opposite his bed, two chairs to the side, and a table sat in the corner with a vase of fresh African tulips, begonias, and delphiniums. The brilliant display of red, orange, pink, and white flora caught his attention. As he inhaled their light, crisp scent, he wondered who had sent the flowers. A card sat beside the vase but he didn't bother reaching for it.

He scrubbed a hand over his face, his frustration rising. Why couldn't he remember the accident or the events leading up to it? Perhaps if he focused on the things he could remember, he could work his way forward.

He recalled his identity. Easy. He'd recognised the name on the tag. Felix Essien. Definitely his name. Son of Chief Aloysius Essien, chairman of Apex Group, and Mrs. Margaret Essien.

Clenching his jaw, he rubbed the back of his neck as anguish burnt across his chest. His mother had died when he'd been eight years old.

Palms pressed against his eyes, he puffed out a relieved sigh as he remembered the woman with the beautiful smile and dark curly hair who had referred to him as 'the apple of my eye.' He never wanted to forget her. Regret knotted his stomach.

These days, he referred to Mrs. Angela Essien as Mother, not stepmother. His father had laid down the rule very early on when she moved in. Mark and Tony Essien were his brothers; he hadn't referred to them as half-brothers since they were boys.

They were all Essiens, family regardless of the blood ties. They stood by each other, no matter what life threw at them.

The Essiens ruled the African financial sector—Kings of African finance, according to Business Times magazine.

As head of Apex Private Bank, Felix reigned over the private banking arm of the Apex Group. Their head office had its base in Lagos, with branches throughout sub-Saharan Africa and other main offices in Johannesburg, Nairobi, London, and New York.

A business he needed to get back to. Leaning forward, he picked up the remote control and flicked the TV on. He found the news channel, hoping to catch up on world events and business news from the past six weeks.

He reached for the jug of water on the bedside table. Anchoring his uninjured left leg, he pulled himself up but winced as a sharp pain shot up his right leg, bound in a cast. Letting out a silent curse, he sat up and poured himself a glass of water from the jug. As he drank, he stared at his injury, wondering how long he would have to wear the cast. He had a business to run and needed to get out of the hospital as soon as possible.

Placing his cup back on the table, he turned just as the most beautiful woman he'd ever seen walked into the room. A slow-building smile curled his lips. The best thing he'd seen all day stood no taller than five-feet-eight, although a couple of inches could be attributed to her print platform sandals. Slender, but with curves in the right places, enough to hold.

Why am I even thinking about holding on to a stranger? She must have walked into the wrong room.

Elegant. The word whispered across his mind.

Smartly dressed in a black, silver-embroidered linen tunic and with dark-blue skinny jeans that clung to wide hips, she had the refinement he liked in a woman without the haughtiness.

She halted at the door, luscious lips parting as her brown eyes widened, her emotions so easy to read. Disbelief. Acceptance. Joy. Then she walked towards him, her lips widening in a hesitant yet glorious smile.

His heart crashed into his ribcage before racing off in a sprint.

"It's true. You are awake."

Her voice drawled akin to a soft velvet whisper, sending warm shivers to all the wrong places in his body as she leaned over and gave him a hug.

Dazed, he lay there basking in her heat. It seeped into his body and her floral perfume tickled his nostrils. Speechless and enthralled, he watched her. She straightened up, took his hand, and held it between her warm, soft, much smaller ones. His heart rate increased, his body's response to her touch unmistakeable.

Desire. Powerful, heart-stopping desire. It coursed through his veins, filling him with the need to hold on to her. Yet, he wanted more.

Frowning, he looked up at her. She moved her coppery-brunette hair back from where it fell over her face. Long dark lashes and curved brows framed her golden-brown, almond-shaped eyes. Her skin looked so flawless he wanted to reach out and touch it; her lips so sensuous he wanted to pull her back down and taste them.

"Happy Valentine's day, Felix. I'm sorry I wasn't here when you woke up. Please forgive me."

As she spoke, tears pooled in her eyes, inciting a sudden need to take her in his arms and soothe her fears. Berating himself, he stiffened his body instead.

What is she playing at?

Angry at himself for responding to her, he withdrew his hand from hers. He missed her soft skin.

Her eyes widened, enquiring and confused. He ignored her and asked the burning question in his mind.

"Who are you?"

Never had three words caused Ebony so much confusion. Without thinking, she fell back onto the chair behind her. Knots tightened her stomach with apprehension as a thousand and one questions filled her mind.

What is going on here? Haven't I suffered enough? Surely, Felix isn't going to resort to punishing me by denying me.

15

She had rushed to the hospital eager to see her husband awake and on his way to full recovery. Walking into the room to see him sitting up after he'd spent several weeks broken and fighting for his life, her heart had sung with joy. She had visited him every day, torn apart to watch him oblivious to his surroundings. To watch the man who had always been strong, fit, and full of life, lying damaged and unresponsive, had broken her heart.

"I...I'm Ebony," she said, and waited for a sign of recognition from him. When none came, his face remaining impassive, she continued.

"Your wife. Don't you remember me?" she asked, her voice rough and just above a whisper as she struggled to keep her emotions in check and stop her stomach churning with fear. When it came to Felix, she could never hide her feelings.

"I'm not married."

Felix's blunt and forceful reply ripped her heart out. *Again.* A shocked gasp escaped her lips.

He lifted his left hand as if to prove his point. Small white tape covered his third finger.

"The medics had to cover the metal up when you went into surgery," she said. "I forgot to take it off afterwards."

His eyes widened as he peeled off the wrapping and revealed the platinum wedding band beneath. He shook his head before looking back at her, his dark brow lifted in an unspoken query.

Ebony lifted her left hand and showed him her matching solitaire diamond ring and wedding band.

"We got married on the thirtieth of December. Remember?"

When he shook his head, she scrambled in her bag with desperation, searching for her phone. Gadget in hand, she turned it on. The screen saver popped up, a picture of both of them on their wedding day.

"Here, see?" If he wanted irrefutable proof, there it lay.

Breath held, she watched for his response.

He stared at the photo with no sign of acknowledgement, his eyes a blank pool of black ice.

She'd seen that cold expression before. The night when everything changed between them. It should have been the best of her life. Instead, it became the worst. The night he'd had the accident.

Pain lanced through her mind. She squeezed her eyes shut and breathed through it. She couldn't let despair overtake her again. She'd been in that black pit before. Never again. Time to move forward, one step at a time.

"Felix, what's going on?" she enquired with a boldness she didn't exactly feel when he failed to respond with answers to her reflective queries.

Frown lines crossed his forehead as he stared out of the window; his mind seemed to be in a faraway place.

Pinching her lips together, she fought the urge to yell for answers in frustration.

Breathe in from the nose and out through the mouth. She practised her calming technique, hands clasped on her lap, waiting for a reply. She had to be patient with him as he recovered from serious injuries.

Seconds ticked away before he turned to focus on her.

"I've lost some of my memory because of the head injury I sustained in an accident that I can't remember, by the way. It's the reason I can't remember you...us...our wedding."

He sounded exasperated, which she understood.

Air whooshed out of her lungs in relief. He wasn't denying her.

His black eyes connected with hers, conveyed an intensity that hinted at other things more sensual. The air died to a halt in her throat as his gaze turned to the darkest onyx, keeping her transfixed on him.

"But if we are indeed married, then surely I'd remember us."

The implication of his words sank into her brain, her body's response instantaneous.

He might as well have tossed a lit matchstick onto a pile of kindle firewood with her body perched at the top. Except these flames weren't turning her to ashes. Instead, her body awakened, a phoenix rising from the fire.

Heat travelled up from her curling toes in her wedge slip-on sandals to her face, setting her whole body ablaze. Heart pounding in her chest, she squeezed her hands together in front of her and tried to calm her quivering body.

This instant lust existed from the first time she'd seen him. One look from him and her body had responded in a wayward manner. Same as today. Despite being in a hospital, he still wielded power over her body.

And he couldn't even remember her! How pathetic did that make her?

With her heart racing, she looked on, entranced, as a lazy smile dimpled his cheeks dusted with stubble. Though she shaved him every morning—she knew how Felix loved being clean-shaven—a shadow of hair always shaded his chin whenever she arrived back the next day. This morning, it gave his rugged face a fierce and sensual edge, making her want to rub her palms against the coarse, short bristles.

The tilt of his smile said he read her like an open book. Could he read her naughty thoughts, too? Her face flushed and she lowered her gaze as annoyance flashed through her mind. She needed to stop falling for his charms.

"Your shy smile is confusing because it implies that I haven't touched you. But if we are married, *ima-mmi*, then we must have had a wedding night, at least, and I know from looking at you now that I wouldn't have been able to resist you."

Her husband at his most dangerous—full frontal charm.

The husky tinge of his words, the bait. His seductive words, the hook. Ensnared, he reeled her in and she couldn't help stealing a glance at him.

Ima-mmi. My Love. She rolled the phrase around in her head, letting its warmth suffuse her heart, cherishing it. The last time she'd heard him use the term of endearment on her seemed like a lifetime ago.

They'd had a different relationship. Since then, he'd made it very clear he didn't care for her in that way. So why did he use the term again now and mess with her head?

The widened smile showing white teeth indicated he knew exactly what he was doing to her, his intent gaze demanding an answer to his implied query.

Then again, he couldn't remember a thing about their marriage. His words suggested hope for them; that he could come to love her. With his memory gone, they would get a second chance. Could they wipe the slate clean and start again?

Could she provide a satisfactory answer without giving away the troubles with their marriage?

"So tell me.... Did we have our wedding night or not?" The stern tone returned as his expression darkened.

"No." The word left her lips as if wrenched from her very soul after cleaning her out. Shame scorched her cheeks and she darted her gaze away. "We didn't have our wedding night. You had the accident on the same evening."

From the corner of her eye, she watched as a brief frown touched his handsome features.

"You mean we got married and we didn't...?" As he spoke, he gave her a slow appraisal from head to toe, spreading the heat of mortification all over her this time.

Why does the ground not open and swallow me up when I need it to?

"Yes. No. I mean—"

Before she could complete her sentence, the door to his hospital suite swung open and Felix's brother, Mark, walked in, followed by his father.

CHAPTER TWO

"Son of a—"

Chief Aloysius Essien glared at his second son as he entered the hospital suite, warning him not to use a foul word in his presence.

"Gun. You are awake," Mark completed with a huge grin on his face as he clutched his older brother's hand and bumped shoulders with him in the familiar hug his sons shared.

"Daddy, welcome." Ebony straightened from the chair and curtsied.

"You were right, my daughter." He patted the girl's shoulder and gave her a benevolent smile.

Felix sat up in bed, propped up by white, linen-covered pillows, his cast-bound right leg elevated on another pillow, the remaining visible evidence of the life-threatening accident he'd endured.

Seeing his son alive and on the road to recovery, Aloysius exhaled in relief.

Mark stepped back, giving him space. Chief stepped forward and clutched his first son's right hand.

"Son, it is so good to see you awake." His grip tightened and his eyes misted over. "You had us worried for a while. I thought we'd lost you."

Felix's expression sobered. "Dad, you worry too much. It'll take more than a little car accident to knock me out."

"You've got that right," Mark cut in, making a joke. "Nothing can damage that hard head of his. I tried enough times when we were kids."

Felix laughed. "Right after I had knocked some sense into your thick skull."

Aloysius allowed himself a smile as his sons bantered with each other, chasing away the worry that had plagued his mind for weeks. At one point, he'd been close to giving up hope when they doctors couldn't seem to do anything to rouse Felix from his coma. He'd even flown in a specialist neurosurgeon from London. Yet, the prognosis had remained the same.

"Keep interacting with him. Talk to him. Case studies show some coma victims can hear conversations."

So they'd carried on visiting him. Ebony had been by her husband's side everyday and sometimes spent the night at the hospital.

Chief Essien glanced over at his daughter-in-law. She stood in the corner, her arms wrapped around her midriff, her lips curled in a half-smile as she watched the brothers chatting. Though he could see her joy at watching the men interact, her defensive posture lay tinged with sadness. Guilt surged through him and he lowered his frame into the chair that Ebony had vacated, masking his shaking legs.

Had he pushed his son too far? Was he responsible for Felix's predicament? The harrowing thought had kept him awake since the accident that nearly took his son's life.

He took another side glance at his son's wife. She hadn't moved from the spot nor tried to get involved in the men's conversation.

"Where are Mum and Tony?" Felix asked.

"Your mother is in Abuja on a women's conference," he replied. "I called her on the way here. She'll be back later today."

"You know what Tony is like—plays all night in the name of work and sleeps half the day away."

Felix's warm laugh filled the room. "As he reminds us, he's a creative and works when his muse works."

"Yeah, if only his muse would actually earn him some money."

"Surely, the restaurant and bar has broken even by now."

"It would do if the boy would actually concentrate on it instead of chasing a pipe dream of wanting to be a movie mogul."

"Enough about Tony," Aloysius cut in. His two older sons always pushed the youngest. "Not everything is about money."

"Says the King of Finance himself," Mark said and leaned against the wall, crossing his right leg over the other at the ankles, his expression amused.

Out of all his sons, Mark always said his mind even when he laced it with a joke. Felix however, internalised things. Always did as a child. He only said things after careful thought and analysis with measured actions. He never bore a grudge. His anger rose slowly and with volcanic effect.

This left Aloysius wondering why his son had deserted his new bride on their wedding night and ended up in a coma. Had he pushed his son too far by demanding he should get married?

Felix had never been pleased with the idea. Their conversation in his office six months ago came to his mind.

Six months earlier.

"Dad, I can't do what you are asking me to do."

Felix paced his father's office in Apex House, the headquarters of Apex Financial Holdings in Victoria Island, Lagos. Walking up and down, he risked scuffing a thin path of his footprints into the plush, hardwearing carpets.

He paused to stare out of the floor-to-ceiling glass windows blocking the full glare of the mid-afternoon African sun. Below, the sprawling urban metropolis busied itself with midday, bumper-to-bumper traffic jams.

His father pictured the wheels turning in his son's head as he took in the full implications of what had just been revealed to him.

Turning around, the younger man carried on pacing.

"The board is requesting this—has been for a long while." Chief spoke in a calm voice from his seat behind his massive mahogany desk.

"We can't delay it any further or you risk losing your position and influence. We have to think about the image of the business. In a time when the world is in economic meltdown, we cannot afford to lose our clientele just because of your personal wish not to get married."

Felix stopped and turned to face the older Essien, patriarch of the family dynasty and his direct boss. Although when it came to running Apex Private Bank, he—not his father—called the shots. His father's words threatened that autonomy.

"I can't let the board railroad me without a fight. They know our reputation. We are the best in Nigeria...the whole of Africa...at what we do. We have proven our pedigree by superbly managing the funds of the wealthiest people of this continent in the past. Despite the financial downturn, our returns are highly competitive and comparable in the market. I am still the same person at the helm. None of that will change." He punctuated his words by slamming one fist into his open palm.

Chief Essien remained calm, nodding as he listened before speaking. "You are right.... We run a prestigious private bank and our clients are nothing if not unswerving, albeit eccentric. They understand that the person at the helm—you," he pointed at Felix before continuing, "have not changed, but they want to be reassured of the stability of the business via the stability of the person in charge. Marriage is synonymous with permanence and commitment. Moreover, your recent escapade in the tabloids has not done your reputation any good." He lifted a newspaper from his desk to emphasise his point.

Bile rose in Aloysius's gut, leaving a bitter taste in his mouth as he recalled the recent scandal played out daily in the tabloid newspapers over the past month. He paid a lot of money to keep a positive image of his family in the press. Still, some things couldn't be avoided.

Wealthy and single young men, his sons originated from a family dynasty that equated to royalty in these parts. Entanglements with beautiful women came with the territory. An occupational hazard of sorts. He'd brought them up on how to court the media and when to avoid it.

Sometimes, the gossip press were thrown bones to keep them off the fleshy news.

However, a few weeks ago, the *Sun People* newspaper had printed an alleged exclusive from a woman who'd claimed Felix had an affair with her, resulting in a two-year old son. The news had been picked up by the popular Lori Booth gossip blog and had spread all over the internet.

Felix had denied it, claiming he'd never seen the woman nor slept with her.

Aloysius had believed him without a doubt. Of all his sons, Felix wouldn't sleep with a woman without caution or remembering. Mark, perhaps. Tony, definitely. He understood his sons' personalities that well.

They'd called in their lawyers and demanded a paternity test.

"But you know the outcome." His son grimaced. "I was vindicated. The DNA test proved the child wasn't mine, after all, and the newspaper has withdrawn the claim, printed an apology, and paid damages. The lady in question only did it out of desperation, I understand. Abandoned by the father of her very sick son, she needed the money to take care of her child's hospital expenses. Whilst I don't agree with her actions, in fact, it was a huge personal inconvenience—" He rubbed the short stubbles on his chin, making a grating sound,"—I understand her reasons. I've arranged through the solicitors to cover the child's hospital bill and to pay a fixed sum into her account to help her set up a business enterprise of her choice, hence getting some positive press coverage, after all."

Aloysius let out a heavy, resigned sigh; his shoulders slumped as he remembered the stress of the event. Felix took a step in his direction, concern etched lines on his forehead.

"I know, son. But the damage to your reputation had already been done. The board feels that if you don't settle down and get married soon, another scandal will be on the cards in the near future. You cannot avoid it; you have to get married. They have given you until the first of January. Otherwise, they will be voting to replace you. I know Petersen is behind this planned coup. We've worked too hard for this business to be left into his hands."

Kris Petersen had been a thorn in their sides since he acquired minority share holdings when another investor sold up suddenly. Aloysius suspected the man waited for an opportunity to vent his ire on the Essien family for past spites. However, he'd never made such a blatant move before.

"What?" Felix stood still and gripped the back of the chair. His body tensed up, frustration making his jaw tick like a time bomb.

He offered a sad smile as sympathy for his son's predicament settled on his shoulders. As first son, Felix bore the brunt of his father's ambitions for his progeny. He'd provided a legacy for his family and their generations through the Apex Group and ruled it like his kingdom. As heir apparent, Felix would be chairman one day, and Aloysius wanted to ensure his son didn't make the same mistakes he'd made in his youth.

"That's just over three months, Dad. Where am I supposed to conjure up a potential wife from in that time?"

The older man bellowed with laughter in his seat, rocking the chair with the vibrations. Felix stared at him, his fists balled in apparent annoyance. It only made him laugh harder, tears seeping from the corners of his eyes.

His son glared at him. "What planet does the board of directors live on? Am I supposed to wave a wand and magic a wife out of a hat?"

His father sucked in a breath and spoke in a sober tone.

"That's where I come in, my son. I have the perfect candidate for you. She is the daughter of one of my good friends, well brought up, with a good background. I can—"

"No way, Dad," he interjected, stepping back with shock as if the man had slapped him. "I can let you run my life. You won't arrange a wife for me. I can choose my own bride, thank you."

He hadn't expected anything less but his father kept an amused expression on his face and waved his hand with flourish.

"If you are sure."

"Of course I'm sure. I'll see you later," his son replied, his eyes gleaming with banked irritation.

When Felix was riled up, he entered the boxing ring to vent his anger. As teenagers, his father had introduced his sons to channelling any aggression into physical activities like sports. Felix and Kola, his adoptive son, had taken to boxing with ease. They remained sparring partners.

A smiled played on Chief Essien's lips. Kola was a graduate of Nigerian Defence Academy and a veteran of the war in Darfur. Though younger, he could hold his own against a frustrated Felix.

Felix grabbed his jacket from where he'd flung it over the sofa and muttered something his father couldn't quite hear.

"What was that?"

"Nothing, Dad." The door swung shut behind his exiting son.

Aloysius leaned back into his chair and allowed the smile on his face to bloom. He'd sowed the seed of marriage into Felix's mind. Better still, he'd led his son to assume he was backing off and allowing him to make his own choice.

His children understood the need for personal sacrifice for the good of the family as a whole. This wouldn't be any different. Moreover, once the seed germinated, it would benefit everyone, including Felix.

Now as he stared at his healing son and Felix's distant wife, Aloysius wondered if that seed hadn't germinated into disaster. Had he matched them incorrectly?

"There are more important things in life." He tugged Ebony out of her reverie until she sat on the arm of the chair beside him with a tentative smile. "Like Felix getting well enough to take care on his wife. The poor girl has been in this hospital every day since the New Year."

Horizontal lines appeared on Felix's forehead.

"Dad, it's okay. I don't mind—" Ebony fidgeted.

Chief Essien forestalled any more words with a wave of his hand. "No. It isn't okay that your new husband should abandon his marital bed on his wedding night to go racing off into the night and nearly kill himself in the process."

He gave Felix a pointed look.

"I'm just going to have a chat with Kola outside."

Chief Essien ignored Mark as he strode out of the room, allowing him to talk to his first son and daughter-in-law in private.

"It isn't okay that you should spend your honeymoon in a hospital with your husband comatose and you worrying yourself. Look at you. Where is the girl I walked down the aisle not two months ago? You look like an echo of the bubbly girl I know."

He squeezed Ebony's clenched hand as she tensed up.

"I don't know what happened that night and frankly, I don't want to know. But we have a rule in this family. Essiens don't turn against each other. We take care of one another. Ebony is a part of this family now, a part of you, Felix. Don't ever forget that."

They both didn't say a word. Ebony stared at her feet, a slight tremor in her hands. Felix stared at the wall, his jaw tightened.

"Do I make myself clear?"

Felix stared at him and nodded. "Yes, Dad."

"Good. Ebony, make sure you don't spend another night in this hospital. Felix is awake now so there's no need to make yourself sick with worry. In fact, tomorrow, take a day off. Go and treat yourself. Do whatever it is you women enjoy. Go shopping. Visit a spa. Whatever. I want you looking like your old self when I see you at the family lunch on Sunday."

She smiled and nodded.

"Right. Now that I know everything is well, I'm going to head back to Apex HQ to organise a press release about your recovery, Felix. Did the doctor say when you can go home?" He stood up and Ebony moved out of his way.

"He said they needed to monitor my progress over the next twenty-four hours. But it shouldn't be more than a few days if all is well."

"Great." He leaned over and hugged his son. "It's good to see you well again, son."

He allowed tears of joy to mist his eyes and a lump wedged in his trachea. Clearing his throat, he straightened.

"I'll see you both soon." He strode to the door.

"Daddy, I'll see you off," Ebony said behind him.

He tilted his head to the side to look at her. Nearly told her not to worry, but the look on her face said she didn't want to be in the room with Felix at that moment. So he waited for her to walk out of the room first before glancing back at his slighted and baffled son.

"Make it right for her, Felix. She'll come around."

His son gave him a nod before he walked out.

Hands braced against the white wall of the corridor, Ebony gulped in a deep breath and released it at a slow rate. Her body vibrated from the effort to stop from crying. Tears welled up behind her eyelids and a huge lump lodged in her throat.

A warm hand settled on her shoulders, giving her a comforting squeeze.

"My daughter, don't worry. All will be well."

How do you know that? she wanted to ask. Instead, she lifted her head and avoided her father-in-law's gaze. The man didn't understand the enormity of the problems between her and her husband.

"Look at it this way." He pulled her close so they stood shoulder to shoulder sideways. "Felix is alive and awake. You have both been given a second chance to fix whatever went wrong. If I know my son, he isn't one to bear a grudge and when he does something wrong, he is usually quick to make amends. So give him a chance to make it right."

"Daddy, it's not that easy. He doesn't even re—" She caught herself before she revealed that Felix had lost his memory. He hadn't told his brother or his father. Not her place to spill the beans.

"He will come around, I assure you. Just promise me you will give him a chance."

"Okay. I promise. If he changes, I will give him a chance." She doubted he would, though. The Felix she'd seen on their wedding night had been intractable, unforgiving.

"Good girl." Her father-in-law smiled for the first time since he came out of Felix's suite.

With him still keeping his hand on her shoulder, they left the cool hospital building into the mid-afternoon sunshine. The weather forecast this morning had indicated highs about thirty degrees Celsius. The scorching heat on her neck confirmed it. Despite spending almost five months in Lagos already, she still couldn't adjust to the heat. She missed the cool temperatures of New York at this time of year.

Mark chatted with Kola in the car park.

On spotting Ebony and Daddy, Kola strode towards them.

"I should get back to Felix," he said. The man had been by Felix's side since the accident and always ensured somebody watched him when he wasn't there. She could never understand the need for so much security. From the first day she'd met Felix, Kola had always been close by.

Almost as if the man felt responsible for Felix's accident. She guessed being head of Essien security put that kind of responsibility on his shoulders. But from what Felix had told her, Kola was a part of their family, not just an employee. He'd grown up as one of Chief's sons, though he wasn't a biological offspring.

"I'll be up in a little while. I'm just going to get something to drink from the cafeteria," Ebony said.

"Okay." Kola headed inside.

Mark and Daddy bid farewell and got into the Dark Cashmere Bentley. As the car left the parking lot, Ebony returned to the building but headed to the restaurant on the ground floor. The new, state of the art hospital had been constructed to cater to the needs of the new, middle to upper class Lagosians in Ikoyi, a leafy suburb of Lagos. The space boasted clean lines and sleek surfaces with modern technology. Emergency generators were set up to deal with power cuts and the staff proved courteous and professional.

Gleaming tables and polished floor greeted her in the cafeteria. She picked up a bottle of Coke from the self-service counter and queued up to pay. After she made her purchase, she found a table and was about to sit when her phone rang. As it happened, she didn't have to dig for it as she'd taken the phone out earlier to show Felix their wedding photo.

The caller ID didn't show up but she didn't mind as she answered it.

"I hear congratulations are in order," a muffled male voice spoke. She didn't recognise it.

"Sorry, who is this?" she asked in confusion.

"This is someone with your interests at heart."

"Tell me your name."

"My name is not important for now. What I have to say is."

Annoyed, she puffed out air. She'd had the odd crank call in the States but none since she moved to Nigeria. She should've expected that reprieve wouldn't last for long.

"I don't have time for this—"

"I wouldn't hang up if I were you. Not if you want your husband to live."

What? She glanced around her as a cold finger of fear slithered down her spine. The people in the café paid her no attention. None was on the phone.

"What do you know about my husband?" she asked in a low voice, gripping the phone tighter.

"I know that he is awake from his coma."

This got her attention. Nobody outside of the immediate family and the medical staff treating Felix knew of his current condition. So who was this man?

"How did you know that?" She stood up, ignoring the bottle of Coke she hadn't even drunk from yet, and raced to the lift foyer.

"How is not important. But I speak the truth, do I not?"

There was something about the man's accent. It didn't quite sound Nigerian and she struggled to place it.

She didn't respond as she jabbed the call button for the lift.

"What do you want?"

"I want to help you."

"Help me. How?"

Hurry! She willed the lift to arrive quicker so she could get upstairs and check on Felix.
I hope Kola is with him.

"I think we could help each other."

She ignored the lift and headed for the stairwell.

"Look. I don't know who you are and I'm not interested in whatever you have to offer," she said as she ran up the stairs.

"Oh, come on, Ebony. I thought you had more backbone. Are you going to let Felix get away with humiliating you like that on your wedding night?"

Her blood ran cold and she stumbled on some steps.

"What are you talking about?"

"I know he walked out on you. Don't worry about how I know. But I can guarantee you, your husband's behaviour is an Essien trait. His father did the same thing to his mother. Essiens do not understand the words 'fidelity' or 'monogamy'."

Panting, Ebony leaned against the wall on the second floor landing and closed her eyes, fighting back the rush of tearful emotions.

"Why are you telling me all this?"

"I can help you get back at your husband for what he did to you."

"I don't want to get back at Felix."

"Don't you? After he humiliated you and broke his promises to you?"

She remembered that night and her anger swelled. She fisted her hand to her side and clenched her jaw. Felix had hurt her more than she'd thought any man could. He'd ripped her heart out of her chest. For the first time in her life, she'd wanted to hurt another human being. Hurt *him*.

Until she'd turned up at the hospital to find him hooked up to so many machines, fighting for his life. And she'd known her wish had hurt him. Nearly killed him. That guilt ate at her ever since.

"No. I don't want to punish Felix."

"How noble and romantic. Let me put it another way, then. How about punishing him in other to save his life?"

"What?"

"If you don't do as I say, you will be responsible for your husband's death. And I'm sure you don't want another person to lose their life on your account, just like your brother and father."

Every cell in Ebony's body froze and she held her breath. This person on the phone knew way too much about her. She couldn't let anything happen to Felix.

"What do I have to do?" Her voice sounded breathless.

"Simple. Ask Felix for a divorce."

She gasped.

"I can't do that."

"Of course you can. Everyone will understand. Your marriage is not consummated and he abandoned you on your wedding night to seek out alternative company. You've been the good wife and stood by him while he was ill. Now you can move on with your life without him."

"You don't understand. Felix and I are not—" She held her tongue, stopping herself from spilling the beans the second time that day. She'd promised Felix never to discuss the circumstances of their marriage with anybody.

"No. *You* don't understand. If you don't divorce him, then I will have to eliminate him. Make your choice, Ebony. I give you one month. Then I want to hear about your impending divorce."

"Why...why are you doing this?" She struggled to speak past the stone lodged in her throat, her body trembling like a leaf in the breeze.

"Retribution. The Essiens owe me and it's time to collect."

The phone line went dead and she slumped to the cold stone floor in a heap.

CHAPTER THREE

He'd married the most beautiful woman he'd ever seen.

Even before Felix woke fully from his sleep in his hospital bed, the thought played over and over in his mind. Whilst he couldn't remember the intricate details of the marriage, he remembered there had been urgency for him to get married—his board of directors had given him an ultimatum. However, the last thing he recalled showed him how he'd still been searching for the right candidate.

Yesterday's events replayed in his mind. Ebony turning up at his bedside, and then Mark and Dad's visit. He hadn't told either of them about his memory loss. They had been worried enough about him and his recovery. Telling them about his amnesia would have compounded matters. He didn't want anybody doubting his competent ability to run his business.

Moreover, he needed to buy himself some time to figure out what had gone wrong. If the media got a hold of that information, the impact on the business would be massive. So he had no choice but to keep it to himself for now.

Well, Ebony knew, too.

"She's a part of you." His father's words yesterday.

The pain in her eyes when he'd refused to accept they were married had roused intense protectiveness within him.

He'd had to reveal the amnesia to her and reassure her he wasn't just trying to be spiteful.

A familiar scent drifted into his nostrils. Sweet and flowery. Ebony. He remembered the way she'd leaned over him, giving him a hug, her warmth and scent playing havoc with his body. Even now, blood rushed south at the memory. He stifled a groan and turned onto his side.

"Make it right for her." More of his father's words.

Ebony had avoided him after his father's visit, and when she returned to his suite last night, it had been only to say good night. Apart from a brief phone call this morning, she hadn't visited him. Dad had ordered her to take a break and enjoy the day. So she was probably doing as the old man had said, retail therapy or beauty regimen.

Acute pain hit his chest and he rubbed it with the heel of his palm.

You miss her. The thought whispered in his mind and he tried to shake it off.

No. He didn't know her, couldn't remember anything about her.

Except that, as soon as he'd seen her yesterday, he'd wanted to hold her, kiss her. Love her.

This time, he let out a low groan and opened his eyes.

A side lamp lit the room in soft, diffused glow, shadows playing in the corners. The curtains covered the window. Behind it would be night sky. The digital clock scrolling across the blank TV indicated the time as 21:33.

The gentle, regular sound of someone breathing in sleep caught his attention. In a darkened corner of the room, Ebony lay curled up in a chair, her arm under her head on the crook of the armrest, the book she'd been reading discarded on the floor. She looked so fragile, so beautiful in sleep. For a moment, he couldn't breathe. Something held his heart in a vise. A smile curled his lips as warmth settled on his shoulders like a blanket. She'd come to see him, after all.

Is this what she had done every day? Sleeping in that chair couldn't be comfortable. She should be at home enjoying the comfort of a bed. Preferably with him in it. His grin widened.

Whether he remembered her or not, they'd gotten married. His wife. His responsibility. He needed to take care of her.

He reached across to the bedside cabinet and picked up his phone to type a text message to Kola.

Where are you?

36

A reply came back almost instantly. *I'm right outside.*

Felix sent another one.

Get someone to replace you immediately. I need you to take my wife home now.

Sure thing. Give me ten minutes.

Felix put his phone back down. He levered himself up, manoeuvring his injured leg with care, until he sat sideways on the bed. Pain throbbed in his leg. He'd been advised to keep it elevated.

However, the wellbeing of the woman in his hospital suite ranked above his personal discomfort.

He hadn't needed his father's chiding tone yesterday to see how exhausted she appeared.

He would have lifted her into his arms but he couldn't put any weight on his injured leg. Instead, he reached down and moved the strands of hair on her face, tucking them behind her ear. He stroked his fingertips up and down her smooth cheek in a gentle caress.

"Ebony, wake up."

She stirred, her face pushing into his hand, a sleepy smile on her face. The curtain of long dark lashes lifted, revealing blurry, golden-brown eyes he didn't tire of watching.

"Felix!" Seeming startled, she bolted upright. "What are you doing? You—you shouldn't be sitting up like this."

Worry lines furrowed her brows as she stared at his injured leg and pushed the hair off her face.

"It's okay. The doctor says I can start moving, albeit slowly." He grinned at her, drifting his hand to her chin and lifting it up so her eyes met his. "Moreover, I've been strapped up in this bed for too long."

She still didn't look convinced. "Are you sure?"

"Of course I'm sure." He patted the space beside him on the bed with his other hand. "Come."

She looked at him as if he was a man-eating lion. He nodded to encourage her and took her hand to help her up. The bed depressed as she settled on it. Their bodies didn't touch. Yet, her heat seeped into his skin, with a strong need to pull her closer. She looked up at him, her eyes a golden pool that fascinated him. In their depths, he could see desire. Something else he couldn't decipher shadowed that emotion.

So many unanswered questions. They wouldn't all be answered today.

"What are you doing here?" He'd ordered her to take the day off. So had his father.

"I know what you and Daddy said." She looked away from him. "I met up with my friend for lunch and I enjoyed being pampered at the spa. But I've been here every day since you've been hospitalised and it felt strange not seeing you."

"But the chair...you shouldn't sleep in it."

Shoulders rose and fell as she looked up at him through her long, dark lashes.

"When I arrived, you were asleep, so I decided to read. I didn't realise I was so tired. I just drifted to sleep." She bit her bottom lip, drawing his attention to it.

The need to kiss her overpowered him. On impulse, he settled a hand on her back, pulling her close. With the other, he lifted her chin and lowered his head to meet hers.

Muscles on her back tensed. He massaged her skin like he would a skittish horse before a game of polo. With gentle brushes, he swept his lips across hers. The sealed, luscious pair called him to mine their depths. Instead, he coaxed and stroked and traced them with his tongue from one end to the other, bidding his time.

He'd caught a glimpse of her banked passion yesterday when he asked about their wedding night. No matter what else went on, they desired each other. Mutual attraction.

With a low moan, she leaned in and opened for him.

As he slipped in, her sweet flavour exploded on his tongue. She tasted of peppermint and vanilla. In the recesses of his mind, the kiss registered. He'd done this before. Tasted her.

A groan rumbled within and he slid his hands around her waist and lifted her onto his lap so that she straddled him.

Whimpering, she rubbed against him, hips canting against hips, supple breasts crushed to his chest.

Needing intimate contact, he ran a palm over her side, skimming the swell of soft breasts down to the hem of her tunic. He lifted it, his hand making contact with smooth, warm skin. Another moan escaped her lips. He swallowed it, loving her sound and taste. Moving his hand up till it reached her breast, he caressed it through the lace of her bra, flicking the already taut nipple with his thumb.

In response, she ground against his bulge.

Sweet fuck!

Fighting the urge to remove her tunic and take her nipples into his mouth, to strip her bare and take her on the hospital bed, he broke off the kiss. They both panted as he took a steadying breath to control his raging body. Her glazed eyes looked lost, her lips parted.

The vibrating phone prevented him from delving back in.

"That'll be Kola ready to take you home." He ran his thumb across her lips.

She stiffened and blinked. Then the shutters returned, her eyes hardening. Hands shoved his chest. He let her go. She scrambled off his lap, turned her back to him, and straightened her clothes.

"That shouldn't have happened." Her whispery voice sounded strained.

Disappointment punched his gut. Scrubbing a hand over his face, he dropped his head and closed his eyes.

"Why?" The one-word query tore from his lips, grated over open sores.

"You said...."

Head lifted and eyes opened, he stared at her stiffened back, her green, gold-embroidered tunic draped over round hips and limbs encased in skinny black denim. Those bum cheeks had cushioned his thighs moments ago. Staring at them now, his arousal spiked.

If he pulled her back into his arms, would she let him spread her out on the bed and taste everything she had to offer?

Not by the way she shunned him with her back and arms wrapped around her mid-riff.

"Ebony." Her name rolled off his lips, an entreaty.

"Felix, I can't do this."

Bending her knees, she picked up the discarded book, her tote, and walked towards the door.

"Wait."

Desperation. Pride. Sheer bullheadedness. Whatever. Something made him stand despite the doctor warning against it without support. Pain shot up his body. Sweat beaded his forehead.

He swayed, grabbed the bar at the bottom of the bed to steady himself.

Ebony swivelled, eyes wide as saucers.

"Felix! What are you doing?"

"I can't let you leave just like that," he gritted past the pain turning his body feverish. "Don't go. Please."

The cooled air from the air-conditioners had no effect on him. Perspiration dripped down his face and back.

"I'll stay. Please sit down."

"You first." He nodded at the chair she'd vacated.

She complied, placing her bag on her lap like some kind of shield to protect against him. At least, that's how it seemed to him as he lowered his body back onto the bed.

A ragged breath whooshed out of him and his eyes watered in relief as the pain receded.

"Excuse me while I inform Kola to hold off."

She nodded as he typed out the message. Phone back on the table, he stared at his wife.

The interested look she'd given him earlier and the passion of their kiss had disappeared. In their place, she eyed him with wry suspicion, as if unsure of what to make of him.

By all accounts and her behaviour, something bad happened between them. Only one way to find out.

"What happened on our wedding night?"

A defiant tilt of the chin, lips pursed in a straight line, and eyes glaring daggers delivered her scathing response.

Cheeks burning, he puffed out in defeat. They needed to talk. He needed to find out more about them together.

"How about how we met? Surely, that's got to be a good topic."

The corners of her eyes softened and she sucked in a corner of her bottom lip. *Result.*

"Please, tell me how we met."

"Okay." She nodded. "First, though, please lay back in bed. You need to keep you injured leg elevated."

He gave his best charming smile. "For you, I will."

She quirked up an eyebrow in surprise, a hint of a smile playing on her mouth.

He pushed back on the bed and lifted his right leg with his hands. She abandoned her bag on the chair and raced to his side. On contact, his skin scorched. He tried to stifle a groan.

"Sorry. Did I hurt you?" She lifted her hands.

"No." The word rushed out of him. Missing her touch, he almost begged for her to place her hands back on him. She stared at him, waiting. "It's okay. You didn't hurt me."

She returned her hands to his leg and helped as he pushed back with the other. With care, she placed the bound foot on the elevated pillows.

"Thank you." He reached out and held her hand when she moved back. "Please sit beside me."

"Felix, I don't think it's a good idea."

"I promise I won't pounce on you again. Scouts' honour," he said, hand on chest.

She smiled and nodded. Taking her sandals off, she tucked her feet under her Buddha-style as she sat on the mattress.

"So tell me, on what auspicious day did we meet?"

41

Smile widening, her chest lifted as she sucked in a steadying breath and then told him.

Five months earlier.

Exhaustion weighed upon Ebony's shoulders. With her tired state of mind came irritability and the penchant for annoyance at the slightest aggravation. She stepped off the plane from a long-haul flight from New York with a huff.

The regulated air of the plane didn't prepare her for the humid wall of heat that hit her as soon as she disembarked and started the walk towards passport control. The controlled air in the terminal still didn't feel cool enough for her non-acclimatised body. Her magazine became a makeshift fan, agitating the tepid air around her face.

She shifted from one leg to another in the long wait to clear immigration, her irritation heightened by a further wait to pick up her luggage. It seemed several flights had landed about the same time, increasing the human traffic in the airport's arrivals.

At last with luggage in hand, she went through customs into the arrivals' lobby, hurrying out to meet with the family driver picking her up.

As soon as she stepped into the busy entrance hall, a man approached her. She swallowed hard and stared, her brain seemingly unable to process embarrassment or shame at the moment as it analysed this specimen of sheer masculinity.

Probably unfair describing him as a mere man. Tall, he stood head and shoulders above everyone around, except for one other man standing next to him. Broad-shouldered, she guessed that underneath his well-cut gray pinstripe suit lay a lean, muscular body. His complexion gleamed like polished brown teak wood and his facial features could've been carved out of a rugged rock wall. She couldn't help picturing him as a descendant of famous African warriors.

Where do I know the face from? He looked familiar but she didn't know him. Features squeezed into a frown, she worked her brain to figure out his identity.

He smiled at her, a decadent curl of full, sensuous lips that promised so much, and her heart thudded in her chest.

Then it hit her. She pulled out the magazine in her bag and looked at the image in the front cover.

Gosh! It's him. Felix Essien—the oldest of the Essien brothers, the kings of African finance, and one of Africa's most eligible bachelors, according to Time magazine.

Here, in the airport terminal, striding towards her with powerful, purposeful steps, he looked straight at her. She bit down the urge to glance behind her and check if someone else stood there.

What could he want with her? Did he hang around international arrivals looking out for his next plaything? Had he chosen *her?*

She snorted in amusement. To her annoyance, her heart rate increased and heat licked her skin as she pictured two bodies tangled in dark silk bed sheets—she and Felix!

Oh, my!

The object of her new, insalubrious dream stopped in front of her, piercing her with midnight black eyes that sparkled like stars.

"Ebony?" he enquired, his smooth deep voice flowing over her like silk.

He knows my name? Even the way he said it reminded her of melted chocolate on ice cream.

What's the matter with me? I'm regressing into a teenage girl on the spot. All because a cover page playboy spoke to me. I must be more tired than I thought.

"And you are?" she replied, injecting impatience into her tone and making a show of appraising him from head to toe.

The best defence is a good attack. All those novels she'd read about feudal Japan now came in handy.

Men like him collected women like trophies. She wouldn't give him a glimpse of what she'd been thinking so he could capitalise on it.

As she regarded his athletic frame from polished black shoes to arrive back to his face, she noticed his sardonic grin, as if he could read her mind.

"Like what you see?" he asked, his dark brow rising and the corner of his lips lifting with wry amusement.

At his words, her ears burnt. *Who needs blusher with men like him around?* Lowering her eyes, she bit her lip.

Blast! Where is this driver?

She had to get out of here before she did something she'd regret later. Exhaustion and not thinking straight wouldn't be good enough excuses for wanting to rip the clothes off the man. *Haven't I learned to keep away from men?* Having dedicated ten years to one man only to find out she didn't know him at all should be a hard enough lesson for anyone.

She needed a warm shower, some fresh clothes, and some home-cooked Nigerian delicacies. Nothing more. She definitely didn't need to stand in the middle of the airport lobby trading words with this tempting, handsome man, or playing mind games with him, either.

But he didn't disappear like she hoped he would.

"You still haven't told me *your* name." She kept her tone dismissive, looking away from him towards the entrance in the hope that her driver would appear anytime now. She wasn't about to give mister playboy here the upper hand. Moreover, she needed to hear him say his name; to confirm what she already believed.

"Felix Essien. But you already know that."

The unruffled voice coupled with its sexy baritone had her cheeks smarting with surprise. Anyone would think he dealt with irritable women every day of his life.

She quirked her brow and he nodded towards her handbag sitting on the top of the luggage on the trolley. She looked at it; the magazine with his photo on the front cover stuck out of the front compartment.

"Oh." She blanched with mortification and stuffed the glossy back in.

Where is that earthquake when I need it? "So what are you, then? Some kind of welcoming committee? Am I the one-millionth person to walk out of the terminal and my prize a reception from the king of finance himself? Should I expect a camera to be shoved in my face any minute?" she rambled on with sarcasm to hide her horror at being caught out with the gossip mag.

Felix chuckled, a real head back from the gut warm and hearty laugh that vibrated through her body.

It became her undoing. Sheer desire pulsed in her core. But this crack in the casing around her heart indicated something more substantial. Something she couldn't allow.

"You could say that, though I haven't been counting, nor did I arrive with a camera crew. I've come to take you home, Ebony."

His face softened when he smiled and his eyes twinkled, making him seem more human, more approachable. She could see why women fell over themselves to be with him. Felix had an effusive charm that could overpower any woman if she didn't tread careful.

"You've come to do what? Take me home? I think you've got the wrong person. Our family driver is picking me up."

As if on cue, something beeped in her pocket. She picked up her phone and recognised the number.

"Hi, Mum, I'm here. I can't find the driver," she spoke into the gadget, holding up her palm to Felix.

"That's what I wanted to tell you. Afam is not the one picking you up today," her mother replied. "Felix Essien is. He should be there already. Can't you find him?"

She stared up at Felix who stood there watching her with eyes that didn't seem to miss anything. Squinting, she squeezed her forehead in a frown as her mind raced.

What's going on?

"He *is* here, standing right in front of me." She turned her back to Felix and took a step away from him. She lowered her voice, concerned. "Mum, what's going on? Why isn't Afam here?"

"Don't worry about it. We'll talk when you get home. I can't wait to see you." Her mum sounded unconcerned, relaxed even.

"See you soon, Mum. Bye." She pressed the end button and turned around.

Felix still stood where she'd left him, his hands folded across his chest, his dark brow raised in a silent query, his pose majestic. A smile tugged at her lips. For sure, he looked the part of a King!

Am I supposed to accept a ride in this man's car? A man I know nothing about except what I've read in business news and gossip columns. Why had Mum arranged for him to pick me up?

Heart thumping in her chest, her stomach knotted with suspicion. She'd never liked surprises. In her past experiences, they all seemed to end with disaster. Closing her eyes, she took a deep gulp of air to calm down.

I just want to get home and rest.

She opened her eyes and picked up her handbag from the trolley.

"It seems I'm going with you after all, Mr. Essien. So lead on," she said, planting a wary smile on her face and bracing her body for the puzzling time ahead.

Ebony bit her lower lip, her hand tightening in the corner of the plush, soft leather car seat as she tried to quell the swirling sensation in her stomach.

Her initial exhaustion has been replaced by something darker and more deeply rooted. An emotion that tore at her soul and twisted her mind.

She never discussed it with anyone or vocalised it. Now it loomed large over her, a monster threatening to swallow her into an abyss.

Tears built up on her eyeballs and she shut her eyes tight, refusing to let them drop.

Face your monster, Ebony. Don't let it overwhelm you.

Deep breaths in. Slow breaths out.

I will overcome.

She opened her eyes and stared out the window through a mist of tears.

Name your monster and conquer it. Ten years ago, she'd learned the phrase. Now she put it into practice and named her three-headed dragon.

Fear. Pain. Guilt.

She had just flown thousands of miles from New York to Lagos, leaving her old, much-loved life behind to come back to a country she didn't want anything to do with. The country that had claimed the lives of her father and brother.

Yet, she had to come because her mother had insisted; her only surviving relative now wheelchair-bound. She loved her mother and couldn't refuse her anything. Also, it being the ten-year anniversary of the accident, her mother wanted to hold a memorial. Ebony couldn't very well miss that, could she?

Now she sat in the back seat of the car with Mr. Felix Essien. More like Lord Essien, the way people ran around to do his bidding. First, there'd been the man who hovered around him—she'd assumed he must be his bodyguard.

Tut! Why did he need a bodyguard, anyway? The man had been quick to take over her luggage trolley without even a look from Felix. Then the driver had been at attention the minute they stepped out into the bright late afternoon sunshine and had opened the door of the vehicle for her and Felix to get in.

Why couldn't her mum have allowed her to take a taxi if Afam proved unavailable? She could have found her way home without fuss. But, oh no! Good old Mum had other ideas. She arranged this little set up on purpose; Ebony could swear it. She could sense when her mother tried to meddle.

She squeezed her face into a frown as the car raced down the highway. Lagos had changed so much since the last time she visited here. Starting from the better-controlled airport terminal, to the road leading to Lagos Island and Ikoyi. The street vendors and shacks she had seen the last time had been cleared out and the streets cleaned. No police checkpoints to extort cash out of motorists. Better still, fully functioning traffic lights regulated the traffic, with cars stopped at red signals. A far cry from the Lagos she remembered.

The hairs on the back of her neck prickled and she knew *he* watched her. On purpose, she'd chosen to look out of the window instead of facing Felix. Her body's response to him had scared her—scratch that—annoyed her. She had no business being attracted to men like him. She'd already been down that road before and paid the price. No more for her.

But you find him attractive, though?

So who wouldn't be attracted to a good-looking man? In his expensive, hand-made grey suit, he looked irresistible, the cut perfect for his well-toned body. He exuded class, sophistication, and power.

Anger coursed through her veins at the way she'd responded to him. Her body had hummed with the awareness of him. Still buzzed at his closeness—the reason she refused to look at him. He'd be able to read it in her eyes, the ability to hide her emotions not her strong point.

"It seems Lagos has changed a lot since I was last here," she said, risking a glance at him through her lowered lashes.

He studied her in return, a knowing smile on his face. Her body tingled with heat under his scrutiny.

"Yes, the Lagos state government has been working hard to improve the environment for its residents in recent years. I take it you are not happy to be here."

She stiffened in her seat and glared at him.

Just great! She'd been sulking so much even Lord Felix had noticed. Not rising to the bait, though, she frowned, instead.

He simply chuckled, a light-hearted laughter that reverberated in the car. Ebony couldn't resist the smile that tugged at her face. Felix had an overwhelming smile and charm. The softened lines made her want to kiss his face.

"So, when was the last time you visited?" he asked, still smiling.

She hesitated before answering. She didn't want to travel back down that road of memories. However, as soon as she'd stepped off the plane, the humid heat, the earthy smell, and the bustling sights had transported her back ten years. She couldn't avoid it. Perhaps talking to a stranger would be cathartic.

"I was last in Lagos ten years ago. My brother, Chidi, and my dad had just been buried—" She choked, biting her lower lip to stop herself from crying as tears stung her eyes. The memories hurt her heart as well as her head. Worse, she felt guilty—responsible for their deaths.

With blurred eyes, she turned towards the window, blinking to stop the tears from falling, not wanting to break down in front of Felix. She inhaled his citrusy, masculine cologne as he leaned closer and put a handkerchief into her hand.

"I'm sorry for your loss. I didn't realise that would've been the last time you visited. I was in London at the time for my masters programme study and missed the ceremony."

A hand settled on her shoulder, moving in a light caress, his warmth seeping into her skin, soothing her. She leaned into the soft leather seat and gazed up at him. Sympathetic dark eyes stared back at her. They had none of the earlier arrogance, which surprised her.

He hadn't come across as the listening kind when she'd first seen him. Not that she was the talking kind. She didn't discuss this topic with anybody, even her closest friends. But she'd been dreading this trip for months. Now, finally here, the apprehension sat like rocks in her stomach. Having someone to listen seemed a good idea, if it would give her some relief.

"It's just so hard being back here. As soon as I stepped off the plane, the memories came flooding back." She spoke with her heart heavy in the dark memories, her head bowed.

"I understand. It couldn't have been easy for you to come back here. If you'd rather not talk about it...." His voice came at her soft and kind.

"I'm all right." She sniffed into the handkerchief.

"Is that so?"

She looked up and saw him smiling, his lips in a tender curve that had her heart thudding in her chest. The hard lines around his eyes softened and his cheek acquired a dimple. Lord Felix had a human heart beneath the fierce-looking exterior.

And she risked losing hers.

"Yes," she confirmed. She couldn't help smiling back, and some of the weight of her emotions lifted. "You know, I refused to return. I swore I'd never come back here. But my mother practically blackmailed me. Mothers, don't you just love them?" She gave a tentative laugh.

"I know what you mean. Parents can be very manipulative. My father goes to extraordinary lengths to get his children to do what he wants sometimes." Felix's warm laughter cheered her up.

"Oh. You don't want to start me on that one. I have stories."

"And so do I."

Why is it so easy to talk to this man?

They both stopped laughing as the electricity between them intensified, drawing her closer to him, daring her to lean into him as she got mesmerised watching his lips. For a moment, it looked like he would kiss her. At the back of her head, a warning light started flashing.

You are on dangerous ground here. Back away.

She did and leaned into her seat, putting some distance between them. "Why are you being so nice to me?"

His intense stare held her riveted for a moment. "Because I, too, have lost a parent. My mother died when I was a boy."

"Oh. I'm sorry," she replied with a compassionate ache in her heart for this man she hardly knew, yet felt a strong connection towards. Her hand landed on his thigh before she realised what she'd done and she withdrew it.

"Thank you," he said, still studying her with an intensity that stopped her heart. "We are here."

She turned and stared out of the window. They'd arrived at her parents' residence in the leafy Ikoyi suburb of Lagos—a large, white, colonial-style house with sprawling gardens. Strange—though she hadn't been in the house for years, seeing it again made her feel like she'd come home. The driver came around and opened the door. Before Felix could get out, she reached out and touched his arm. He turned back to her.

"I...I just wanted to say thank you for listening and understanding. I know I wasn't on my best behaviour earlier. Thanks for not judging me."

"You're welcome. Anytime you want to unburden, here's my card. Call me. My personal number is on the back." He flashed white teeth, passing her his black, gold-embossed business card, and she smiled in return.

"Thanks, I'll bear that in mind."

Feeing less anxious, she turned and stepped out with a smile on her face. Maybe this trip home wouldn't be as bad as she'd imagined.

The image of a woman sitting next to him in the back seat of his car floated in Felix's mind as he sat in his hospital bed trying to remember. Shoulders and back stiff, her gaze focused on the scenery whizzing by the car as they sped towards the island and their final destination, Ikoyi. Her coppery brown hair had been tied back in a knot, giving him full view of a smooth neck column that fascinated him. A steady pulse beat at the base of her neck. He squeezed his fingers into a fist, fighting the impulse to touch her skin.

The present blended with the past. He remembered his response and thinking he'd met a goddess, remembered the swarm of emotions on her face and feeling like he wanted to hold and never let her go.

Roses. Jasmine. Musk. Her perfume drifted in the air.

Closing his eyes, he took a deep breath, drawing her scent into his lungs and setting his veins on fire. It took an effort not to groan out loud. He clenched his teeth.

Instant attraction. No other explanation for the breathtaking immediacy of his need for Ebony. A craving eclipsing anything he'd ever felt for any other woman. The sensation stayed with him now while the memory faded into a haze as he struggled to recall more.

He opened his eyes and stared at her sitting inches away from him.

"From what you say, we had something good to start with, didn't we?" Uncertainty laced his query.

"We did," she answered in a rueful voice.

"Then give me another chance." Determination and purpose settled on his shoulders.

"What?"

He'd sworn he would never get married because of his parents. Now, regardless of the circumstances surrounding his marriage, he wanted a chance to make it work.

"I don't know what happened. Whatever it is, I want the chance to make amends."

Shaking her head, she slid off the bed. Desperate, only his promise not to pounce on her stopped him from reaching for her.

"If you're not going to give me another chance, what is the alternative? We can't go on like this."

Spinning around, she caught his gaze. "There is one option."

Cold, bold brown eyes didn't waver. He read the message in them.

"Divorce? We haven't had a chance to make this marriage work."

"You made your opinion of this marriage very clear at our wedding." The disdain in her voice rivalled the chilly Harmattan winds from the North.

He puffed out air in frustration. The night would haunt him forever and he couldn't remember a damned thing!

"We've only been married two months." He tried another tactic.

"Six weeks. Five days. Twelve hours...." She glanced at the diamond and platinum link watch on her wrist.

He couldn't help grinning. There had to be hope for them. "You've been counting."

A small smile played on her lips. "Only because that's how long you've been in this hospital."

"I'm sorry." He took a chance and reached out for her.

She stared at his hand as if it was a king cobra.

"If you give me the chance, I'll be the best husband ever." His chest constricted as he drowned and waited for her to throw him a lifeline. "I promise, I won't cheat on you. I won't lie to you. I'll give you the finest things money can buy. I will take care of you." *And I will love you.*

Pushing the thought aside, he didn't say the last bit. It had to be the reason he was in this predicament. Married when he'd never wanted to be before he met Ebony. Yes, the board at Apex Private Bank had given him an ultimatum about getting married.

Knowing his history, he would never have married Ebony unless he loved her. It would explain this desperation he felt to keep her in his life. What else would it be?

Disbelief flickered in her gaze. Why would she doubt him? What did he do to deserve such suspicion?

"I swear—"

"No. Don't swear."

Brought up a Catholic, swearing on anything holy was forbidden. Yet, he would've sworn on his life.

"I'll give you one month."

Breath rushed out of him, and he ran a palm over his face. One month should be plenty of time. God willing, he would have his memories back by then.

"Good." He kept his hand outstretched, palm open. "Come, *ima-mmi*. We need a kiss to seal the deal."

This time, she took his hand, and when he tugged, her chest descended across his. Fisting his fingers in her hair, he claimed her lips as fiercely as he'd wanted to the first time. No finesse. Just passion and urgency as their tongues tangled.

Their second kiss as far as he could recall, her taste already an addiction filling his body with granite need.

Murmurs of pleasure called him to explore the pliant curves crushed against his torso. Instead, he broke the kiss. Panting breath feathered his face in warm puffs.

"Go home. Get plenty of rest. Prepare yourself for me." He nibbled her soft lips. "We have a lot of catching up to do, starting with our wedding night."

The sound of her hitched breath and the sight of her lust-filled eyes widened his grin. Passionate Ebony had returned. He would keep her hot and wanting; she wouldn't think about leaving him.

Stroking his knuckles across her cheek, he pressed his lips against hers one final time before releasing her.

She wobbled on feet and straightened.

With a grin plastered on his face, he called Kola. "She is ready."

CHAPTER FOUR

Prepare yourself for me.

Ebony's head echoed with Felix's instruction as she sat at her dresser two days later. A thousand butterflies fluttered in her tummy while her blood seemed to have turned into fizzy champagne.

She clutched her chest, heart thumping a fast, erratic beat. Had she ever been so excited and nervous at the same time?

"I am the epitome of serenity," she chanted and closed her eyes, letting the peaceful sounds of her environment permeate her mind.

Birds tweeted, insects chirruped, wind whistled through the trees in the garden. Tranquillity. One of the benefits of living in a private cul-de-sac on a vast mansion where your nearest neighbour's noise couldn't reach you, nor did you get any traffic rumble.

Opening her eyes, she busied herself with getting ready and looking her best. A visit to her hairdresser the previous day had left her straightened hair soft and silky. Now with blow dryer and heat tong in hand, she styled it into waves cascading down her shoulders in waves. The auburn highlights set off the amber of her eyes.

Felix would be home today; the doctors had given the all clear. He could go home as long as he rested and took things one day at a time. His physiotherapy appointments had been scheduled. Being in familiar surroundings would help to jog his memory, the doctor had said.

Gladness lifted her spirits. Having Felix home would be the answer to long prayers at his bedside each day he'd been unconscious.

She hadn't received any further phone calls from the strange man who had threatened her, so she dismissed it as a crank call and shifted it to the back of her mind. Moreover, there was no need adding to Felix's troubles. He had his hands full with amnesia.

At dawn, she'd risen, eager to ensure everything was laid out as planned for his arrival. She'd instructed the domestic staff on what she needed the previous day. Housekeeper, gardener, gateman, even the part-time laundry boy that came in twice a week—all stood before her and she'd laid out her instructions.

Today, the sweet scent of fresh flowers filled the house, surfaces gleamed with polish, garden hedges looked trimmed, all the cars were washed, and Felix's favourite food had been cooked.

Ebony now needed to look the part of the lady of the house. A woman looking forward to her husband's homecoming.

In truth, she didn't need to pretend. As much as the unknown future scared her, excitement at seeing Felix home overwhelmed every other emotion.

The determination in his eyes when he'd promised to be the best husband ever convinced her of his intentions. His sincerity and openness has been surprising but welcomed. He'd begged her. Something he'd never done before. So unlike the ruthless and business-driven man from before the accident.

"This is your second chance," his father had said.

Perhaps the accident and Felix's memory loss provided the opportunity for them to let go of the past and start again. Perhaps this new Felix would care for her.

Perhaps he would love her one day....

If it would heal the bitterness surrounding her heart, she would give them a chance.

And if the way he'd kissed her indicated what lay ahead, then she would embrace it.

Cheeks burning, she fingered her lips, remembering the caress of his fingers and mouth, the sweep of his tongue, the nip of his teeth. The grind of his hips.

"Oh, God!" she moaned out loud and squeezed her thighs together.

Since the kiss, two nights ago, he hadn't touched her.

Well, he had. A feather peck on the cheek, a gentle squeeze of the hand, a brief hug—fleeting gestures had left her craving more of him.

Ironic, since she'd spent six weeks since their marriage with no sexual stimuli.

Felix awoke, held and kissed her, turning her into a walking hormone bomb. Now she hoped her husband would go back on a promise he'd made before their marriage.

At the full-length mirror, she studied her appearance. The multi-print lace and organza dress with intricate gold embroidery flowed and shimmered over her body like a waterfall.

Flat-heeled diamante sandals and gold nail varnish glittered on her feet. She preferred walking barefoot in the house, but not on a special day like today.

Straining, she listened out for any indications of a car arriving. Nothing. She picked up her phone from the dresser. She'd wanted to go to the hospital and bring Felix home. He'd told her not to, and for the last few days, had restricted her visiting time.

One thing the knock in the head hadn't taken away was his commandeering attitude. Man-in-charge had returned full force.

A smile played on her lips. Truth be told, she found the take-charge Felix irresistible. In a country where people dragged their feet without reason sometimes, Felix could get things done with a snap of his fingers. Being Mrs. Felix Essien had its perks. Doors opened even before she asked them to be opened.

What if he finds out the truth? What if he remembers?

She sucked in a breath and closed her eyes.

"I can't dwell on it," she muttered to herself. "Not now. I'll cross the bridge when I get to it."

A knock at the door made her jump, eyes flying open.

"Who is it?"

"*Oga* Felix is here," Bisi said from the other side of the closed panel.

Thud. Thud. Thud. Her heart raced. *He's home.*

Pushing aside her worry, she flung the door open.

Bisi stood on the landing at the top of the stairs with a shy smile.

"Make sure everyone else is out there to greet him," Ebony said as she smiled.

"Yes, Aunty. They are already waiting."

"Good. Let's go down."

Bisi raced ahead. Ebony tried for a dignified descent and quelled her anticipation.

Outside, the household staff, in smart, clean, and ironed uniforms, stood in a row to greet their master as the driver unloaded the boot of the car.

Felix straightened out of the car and Kola handed him a crutch.

She had been expecting him, but seeing him standing there, in loose cargo pants and a t-shirt, the handsome virile man she'd fallen in love with so evident, she couldn't help the tears that pooled in her eyes, the last time he'd stood on this same portico a lifetime ago.

With a smile on his face that sent her heart tripping over, he held out his free hand towards her and she went to him.

Wrapping her arms around him, she inhaled the spicy mix of Felix and his aftershave. Relief skittered over her skin, joy curling lips pressed to his shirt.

"Welcome home," she breathed against him. He pulled her even closer, giving her a firm squeeze before letting go. They hadn't seen each other in twenty-four hours. Had he missed her? She stepped back and looked up at him. The intensity of his dark eyes snatched air from her lungs.

"It's good to be home." He faced the staff. "Thank you, all."

"You're welcome, sir," they replied in unison.

"Bisi, how are you?"

"I'm fine, sir."

"Good. Your madam—"

Ebony elbowed him in the rib. "They don't address me as madam. I prefer aunty."

He beamed a charming smile and started again. "Your aunty tells me you are taking evening classes. Are you enjoying it?"

"Yes, sir. I love it, sir."

"Great. Chima, how about you? How is school?"

Chima, the part-time laundry boy, studied at University of Lagos. The job earned him money to supplement whatever his parents gave him for his schooling.

"Great, sir. Everything is going great. Thank you."

"Kwame, the garden looks fantastic. How is your family?"

"Everybody is fine. Thank you, sir."

"How about you and your family, Abdul?"

Abdul served as the day watchman. At night, he was supplemented by Kola's security team.

"Everyone is fine, *oga. Na gode*." *Thank you.*

"Thank you, everyone," Ebony said. "Chima, please take the bags in. Bisi, set up the table. I'll be in the kitchen shortly."

The staff nodded and dispersed to carry on with their duties.

"Come inside, out of the heat." She tugged on his free hand. Since the moment he had woken from his coma, the rapport between them had grown stronger each day, which reminded her of the easy friendship they'd develop when they first met. He could read her with ease and knew her thoughts before she'd voiced them.

When they walked into the grand hallway, she stopped and turned to him. He still held onto her hand, lifting it and brushing soft lips against knuckles. A wayward shiver passed through her body.

Tilting her head to the side, she expected to see Kola following behind. Instead, the car outside headed back down the driveway to the wrought iron gates.

"Where is Kola going? Isn't he staying for lunch?" she asked, eyes widening in surprise.

"I sent him to pick something for me from Apex Towers. He'll be back soon."

"Okay." She wrinkled the corners of her eyes. "I hope that doesn't mean you're planning to get back to work right away."

"Not right away." Amusement dance in his midnight eyes.

Cheeks flushed, a slow smile tugged her mouth.

"What would you like to do first?" She had to swallow to get the words out. "Have a rest, freshen up, or eat?"

"Does a rest involve you joining me?" The corners of his lips crinkled in teasing curve, the tone of his voice promising such decadent pleasure.

Gosh, she'd missed that smile. Her body pulsed to life, yearning for fulfilment, arousal beading her nipples.

Get a grip. Lady of the House, remember? Not Sex Bomb.

Swallowing, she swatted his arm. "Felix, stop kidding. You know we can't. Your leg."

"I know of ways we can—No?" He laughed when she fixed him with a no-nonsense look. "Okay, then. I'll freshen up before we eat."

"Good," she said cheerily and started walking again. Her errant body would have to get used to being unfulfilled. "I had the downstairs guest suite prepared for you."

"Why?" He stopped walking, a frown on his face.

"To save you from climbing the stairs, of course."

"And keep me away from you for a few more days? I don't think so, *ima-mmi*."

"But—"

"No buts. I know you are thinking about my welfare but I need to think about *our* welfare, too." He tugged her closer and fixed her with an intense, all-knowing stare. "Do you want to spend another night away from your husband? Honestly?"

How could he have known her deep thoughts?

She shook her head, telling him with her eyes and her entire being that she didn't want to be apart from him any longer. "No."

"Then it's settled. We are not spending a night apart any more. And I'm sleeping in *our* bed." He grinned wickedly at her and started walking towards the stairs, his crutch clicking on the marble floor.

He'd meant it. They were going to actually live together as man and wife in the true sense. As she watched him silently take the stairs one at a time, concern for Felix overtook all else. Though his facial expression remained intractable, it was obvious he felt pain as he navigated each step. When he reached the top of the stairs, he paused briefly by the balustrade before walking into the master suite.

She followed him into the room. He took a seat on the settee, his face looking strained, and sweat glistening on his forehead. Stubborn man! If he wouldn't accept help, then she would have to find another way of helping him. He certainly wasn't going back downstairs anytime soon.

"I'm going to arrange to bring lunch up. We can eat here," she said, hands on hips.

"Not before this." He took her arm and pulled her onto the settee. She fell onto his hard lap.

"Felix!" Stunned, she wriggled, trying not to sit on his injured leg. What was he up to?

"Stop wriggling," he growled. She froze as his mouth descended on hers.

Resistance proved futile. Any thoughts about his leg fled her mind. She surrendered to his sensual assault, heat spreading through her body. With his hands on her nape and holding her in place, the other roamed her body, leaving a trail of tingles in its wake. A quiver travelled through her. She arched her body closer to his, a moan escaping her lips as she got lost in sensation.

When he moved his lips downwards, his tongue licking the pulse on her neck, she tilted her head back to give him more access. Her core ached with need. Nobody else brought out this same level of awareness in her. He stopped, lifting his head up. She whimpered in disappointment, her hand moving to pull his head back down. She looked into his eyes. His stare of pure desire snatched her breath away.

"I haven't been a good husband, have I?" he asked, his voice laced with sadness.

His question caught her by surprise. Where did that come from? Could he be having regrets about their marriage already?

"You haven't had the opportunity to be a husband. You can't blame yourself. It's not as if you planned the accident." She shrugged with nonchalance she didn't feel.

"Regardless, I plan to start making amends straight away. The question is, do you want to remain married to me? I pray that you say yes because there are so many things about you I want to find out."

Taken aback again, Ebony watched his face closely. His eyes confirmed his sincerity. There was nothing else she wanted more right now.

"Yes. I want to stay married to you."

He pulled her back into his arms, his passionate kiss knocking the breath out of her body. When he released her, she remained panting.

"Now for lunch. Unless you'd rather we followed this through to its natural conclusion. I'm here to do your bidding, *ima-mmi*." He winked at her, patting her bottom.

"Oh, you are such a rogue." She smiled at him and took a step back, allowing him to get up and walk to the bathroom. When he shut the door behind him, she raced downstairs, eager to organise lunch.

Felix sat at his desk in his home office, scanning the laptop screen open before him while he caught up on his emails and the documents his executive assistant had sent him. He might be unable to physically go into his head office but there existed no reason he couldn't keep in touch with activities via email and phone.

Moreover, the quarterly meeting of the Executive Board of Apex PB convened in a little over a month's time. His ability to head the division would be back on the agenda if he didn't demonstrate his capability as to lead the bank. According to the minutes of the last meeting in January, the vote to rout him from the position had only been deferred, and not squashed, due to his accident as they awaited his recovery.

An act that would seem merciless to outsiders. Still, he didn't begrudge the Board anything. Simply business. Nothing personal. Just accountability.

Billions of dollars worth of clients' money flowed through the accounts of their clients. Ultimately, the buck stopped with him.

A knock on the door roused him from his reflections. "Come."

He looked up from the screen and leaned back into his soft-padded oxblood leather chair.

The door opened and Kola stood at the threshold. "I'm just about to head home. Do you need anything else before I go?"

"Aren't you staying for dinner?" Felix asked as he frowned.

Kola stepped in, shutting the door behind him. "I don't think it's a good idea."

"Why not? Is this about Ebony?"

"No. Of course not." His security chief stood before his desk, both hands behind his back, legs wide apart in a relaxed pose. "I just think it might be a good idea for the two of you to...you know...hang out together...alone. No disrespect, brother."

He must have fucked up pretty bad for Kola to interfere. Usually, the man didn't intrude in his private matters. Although he'd been raised with the rest of the Essien brothers, he'd had a rough childhood and had been rescued from the streets by their father. However, since Kola resigned his commission in the army, he'd been closed up and Felix was certain he fought some horrific personal demons left over from what he'd encountered in Darfur. Felix only hoped that one day, he would share his personal experience with him.

Felix nodded. "Before you go, I've been meaning to talk to you about the accident. Please sit."

"Sure." He sat in one of the leather armchairs in front of the desk.

He'd gone online to search for news quips about his accident. Sure enough, there were reports about it. Apparently, he had been travelling alone in his car at night when a heavy-goods vehicle had crashed into him at a junction, swiping his car off the road into a ditch. The truck driver had lost control of his vehicle. Kola, who'd followed him in another car, had been first on the spot. Felix's car lay turned upside down, his foot trapped in the wreckage. From the pictures, he'd been lucky he survived the accident. His Bugatti Veyron had been mangled, a total write-off.

"I told you in the car that I don't remember anything about the accident." He'd thought it important to tell him. The man was responsible for his security. "But I'd really like to know what happened that night. Why did I leave this house so late? Where was I going, for goodness' sake?"

"I really wish I had the answers for you," Kola said. "I'd just dropped you guys home after the wedding party. You were quiet during the drive back. I thought it was just exhaustion. When you both went inside, I was chatting with Freddy from the night team when I heard raised voices inside. I would've headed off home but hearing the two of you arguing on your wedding night and I just couldn't leave until I was sure everything was okay."

Felix rubbed the back of his neck as embarrassment heated his cheeks. Being a private man meant he hated others overhearing his conversations, especially a heated one as Kola described. But he needed answers so he asked, "What were we arguing about?"

"I couldn't hear the sentences, just loud angry voices." He lowered his head. "Then you came tearing out of the house in rage and yelled at the boys to open the gate for you. You drove that car out faster than I'd ever seen you do before. If that truck hadn't hit you, you would've probably hit a ditch all by yourself or another road user."

Felix swore out loud.

"Yep. You raised one hell of a shitstorm that night." Kola's jaw tightened. "I walked into the house to find Ebony crying her eyes out. Still, I had to leave her to chase after you. Luckily, the tracking device on the Bugatti showed me which direction you were headed. But by the time I got to you, it was too late. I can tell you it was no fun finding you unconscious. I had to put you in the back seat of the Range Rover and drive you to hospital myself. But the toughest part was calling Chief to say you were in hospital. I never want to do that again."

"You saved my life." He scrubbed a hand over his face, regret making him uncomfortable. "Thank you."

"Don't mention it. We are like brothers, after all, and your safety is my job."

You're supposed to protect me from others. Not from myself. The unspoken thought worried Felix, but he nodded.

"If that's everything, I'm going to head off now." Kola stood. "Freddy is on duty tonight and he's happy to provide any extra help you need in getting upstairs." Amusement glimmered in his eyes.

"What's so funny?" Felix asked.

"Nothing."

Felix raised a brow.

"Just that I overhead Bisi and Chima discussing the lack of use of the master suite bed. Apparently, Ebony hasn't been sleeping in it."

"What is that supposed to mean?" Uncomfortable, he shifted in his seat as anxiety knotted his shoulders. "Where has she been sleeping?"

"I had to tell them off for gossiping but Bisi revealed Ebony has been sleeping in one of the other rooms upstairs."

"Oh. Okay. Thank you again."

"Sure. If you need me tomorrow, just call and I'll come over."

"It's the weekend. Take a break. You deserve it."

"No can do, bro. You know I'm shadowing you until you're back on both feet," Kola said as he headed for the door. "Good night."

"Night." Elbows on desk, Felix lowered his head onto his hands and rubbed his eyes.

Shouting and arguing with Ebony? Ebony sleeping in a different room? Gossiping staff. His home was disintegrating. Something he'd never wanted to happen. He'd lived through a disintegrated home as a child. He inhaled sharply as the raw pain renewed.

Arguing parents. Parents sleeping in separate rooms. Days on end when his father wasn't home. His mother had claimed he had travelled. Yet, he'd caught his mother sobbing in her room.

Kola had found Ebony crying, too.

He reared back, fist clenched, and stared out of the window into the garden. Manicured lush lawn, trimmed purple hibiscus hedges, pink bougainvillea winked in the dusk light of the setting sun as the gardener watered the plants with the hose pipe.

Usually, he loved the outdoor space. Today, the view didn't lighten his heavy heart. While he had a business to worry about, the affair with his wife needed his urgent attention. At least they'd started on the right road.

He'd had lunch earlier with Ebony. Her eyes had been lit up with what he assumed to be joy, passion, and something else. At the time, he'd just been happy to see her smiling and chatting, looking like she was enjoying her food.

She had gone to what seemed like great trouble to make him comfortable and had fussed over him. He expected to feel uncomfortable, or even awkwardness, around her. But there lay none. They interacted like he'd known her his whole life. Knew what she could be thinking by the way her eyes sparkled or the tilt of her head. There existed a familiarity about her he couldn't pinpoint. Like she was a part of him that had always been here. Each time she looked at him, he could see the love in her eyes.

That's it! Ebony loved him! Had she always done so? Her daily vigils at his bedside certainly showed she cared about him. Did he love her in return? If love proved the overwhelming need to take care of her, to spend the rest of his life devoted to her happiness, then he did. He'd certainly never felt that way for anyone else. Could that be why they'd gotten married?

Today, though, nothing about her had been withdrawn. Seeing her as she stepped out of the front door to greet him had warmed his heart. She'd looked so radiant, her dark skin glowing in the sunlight and her smile glorious. He'd felt like being favoured by a goddess. The sun had caught on the coppery strands of her hair, turning it into a cascade of flames tamed by the brown strands. Having her in his arms had been like heaven, her now familiar scent surrounding him, welcoming him home. She belonged to him and him to her. His body's wild reaction to her had been instantaneous. When he'd kissed her in their bedroom, it had taken all his control to stop at just kissing.

His body stirred again. He needed to go to his wife. Shutting down his laptop, he stood and went in search of her.

Ebony walked out of the en-suite bathroom and stopped. Felix sat on the bed, taking his shirt off. At the sight of the broad shoulders, taut pectorals, and rippling bicep muscles, her breath caught in her throat and a warm shiver crept up her back. Fascinated, she stared at him with undisguised hunger, lips parted, body flushed.

He tossed the shirt aside and their gazes met. His cheek dipped with a dimple, his smile oh-so-sexy.

Lava pooled low in her belly. She swiped clammy hands over the silk negligee covering her thighs.

What was the matter with her? Felix had been injured, sex probably the last thing on his mind. She needed to concentrate on making him comfortable.

"Can I help you with something?" she asked, keeping her tone jovial. But her face heated up when his lips curled in a wicked grin.

"Sure, you can. Come here." His deep, husky voice sent her heart racing with anticipation. Her awareness of him racked up to scorching level.

Legs trembling a little, she walked over to him and stopped at arm's length. Desire filled his eyes, turning them into fiery onyx. An ache settled in her core, a need for him to kiss her again, to feel his hands setting her skin ablaze. She wanted to taste him, to touch him. Yet, she hesitated.

"What would you like me to do?" she asked, not sure if he wanted help with his trousers, unable to keep her eyes away from his stomach muscles tapering into them. She tried to keep her thoughts on what needed to be done. The loose-fitting cargo pants were probably the only things he could wear with the plaster cast on his ankle. With zippers at the sides and on the hems, it could come off easily

"Come closer," he demanded in a low, growling voice.

CHAPTER FIVE

At his command, Ebony braced her quivering body. Took another faltering step towards Felix until she stood between his thighs and their firmness pressed against her legs.

This man, her husband, stared at her with smouldering gaze as if he unlocked his soul and laid it bare for her to see. The thudding of her heart against her ribs increased.

Was it really wrong to succumb, to let him fulfil what his eyes promised, what she wanted? After months of misery and grief, was this little respite not unwarranted?

After all, he belonged to her, legally, at least. She wanted to claim him and be claimed in return. For the past two months, she'd felt like a possession abandoned on the lost property shelf and yet with an owner's tag. Discarded.

Had her luck finally changed? Would she be returned to a place of pride at Felix's side?

Without a word, he reached out and tugged the belt of her short, burgundy silk robe. She held her breath, expectation bubbling through her. The intensity of his gaze burned her up. The robe fell loose, exposing a matching silk negligee underneath.

Warm, rough palms slid down her neck, pushing the robe off her shoulders. It fell in a pool of silk on the intricately designed Oriental rug. He ran his hands up and down her arms; goose bumps skittered over her skin.

"I'm going to learn your body." His husky voice washed over her in awareness. "Every curve, every dip, ever contour, every swell. What makes you gasp with pleasure, what makes you sigh with satisfaction."

Long fingers traced her face in a gentle caress and then slid downwards, leisurely, to her neck, the valley between the swell of her breasts, over and under her breasts, flicking her already hardening nipples. The friction he created with the silk fabric against her sensitised skin sent a multitude of sensation thrilling through her body. She let out a soft mewl.

"And when I'm done, you will be screaming my name in ecstasy. Would you like that, *Ima-mmi?*"

Yes! Working her heavy tongue in suddenly dry mouth proved useless. Lowering her lashes briefly as she struggled to control her choppy breathing, she nodded instead.

His hands moved further down, gliding over her flat, contracting stomach muscles, hips, trembling thighs, and finally coming back up to rest on her waist.

With his thumbs skimming the under swell of her breasts, his hands bunched up her short negligee, gathering the hem to her waist. He paused and stared at her belly button.

Her skin tingled as he leaned forward and pressed soft lips against the dip on her tummy, then pink, rough tongue slid out and licked the spot.

Knees trembling, she clutched his shoulders to keep upright. Sensation pooled between her thighs at his tender yet erotic gesture.

"I want to see the rest of you. Raise your hands."

She complied and he pulled her negligee over her head and dropped it to join the robe.

Exposed and vulnerable, she stood silently, trembling both with uncertainty and expectation. She couldn't hide her physical and emotional reaction to him.

Leaning back, he surveyed her with unconcealed longing.

Tell him. This was not part of your arrangement with him.

Doubt warred with desire. When Felix's memory returned, he would surely blame her for deceiving him. For letting him do this. He'd sworn he'd never touch her like this.

Still, she wanted—needed to feel like a cherished woman after all the trauma. Ached with her heart and body for him—his words, his touch, and his love. She would take whatever he offered, even temporarily.

He held either side of her head, lifting her chin up so her yearning golden eyes met his scorching black ones. Her need to connect with him nearly knocked her over.

"You are beautiful," he uttered huskily and tugged her closer.

She tumbled into him. Any reservations she had dissolved with the kiss, his mouth taking possession of hers. She clung to him, her hands on his shoulders. His hands played with her breasts, tweaking the already taut and sensitive nipples.

Awareness ratcheted up within her—of Felix, his hands, his tongue, his body, his heat, his smell, all of it an intoxicating foray that broke down her walls. She succumbed, giving what he demanded and taking all that he gave.

A trail of heat followed his hand on her skin as it travelled downwards, skimming her sensitive inner thighs, finally stopping at her apex. Her womb contracted with expectation. She moved her legs wider apart, eager for his touch to her inner recesses.

Melting, burning up, she'd craved his touch for so long, and she moaned her impatience when he didn't delve in immediately at her body's invitation.

Palm pressed against her mound, he broke the kiss. Panting, she opened her eyes to find a smile of pure masculine pride and hunger on his face.

With his left hand braced on her back, holding her up, his right hand parted her inner folds. Fingers slid against her slickness, circling but not touching where she needed him most. Her breath caught in her throat, her body flushing.

Delight coursed over her when his mouth captured a sensitive nipple and sucked gently. His thumb flicked her swollen nub and her juices coated his digits. She gasped with pleasure as his fingers filled her expanding core. Grasping his shoulders and lost in sensation, she rode his hands as he pumped his fingers into her, tilting her head back in ecstasy and crying out his name.

Unexpectedly, he swept her up and laid her flat against the pillows on the bed. His desire- filled gaze skimmed her body.

"Tonight is about you. I want to taste you. To feel your pleasure in my mouth. To watch you come apart."

The mixture of her mind-blowing orgasm and his adoring words overwhelmed her with emotion. Tears misted her eyes and her throat clogged up.

If this is a dream, I never want to wake up.

"This is no dream, Ebony." His knuckles brushed her left cheek.

She squeezed her eyes shut, uncomfortable for speaking her thoughts out loud.

"Look at me."

Warm air feathered her face. She lifted her lids at his demand to find his face only inches from hers.

Onyx eyes burned with passion, his voice gruff. "I need you to trust me."

Arm braced on both sides of her body, he lowered his head and sealed their lips in a kiss filled with reverence and affection. Less insistent. Slow and gentle.

Sandwiched between the plush satin bedspread and the rock hardness of Felix on top of her, she basked in the decadent caresses he extended to the rest of her writhing body.

Arousal fired up in her veins. This wasn't just a physical need for fulfilment but an emotional longing to connect with the soul inhabiting his body. Never had she felt this longing to be completely consumed.

Felix worshiped her body with his hands, mouth, tongue, teeth. With each lick and nip, each swipe and caress, he studied her expression as if learning what pleased her.

Fingers clutched the sheet, teeth biting her bottom lip as he slowly drove her insane with feverish need.

His indulgent kisses peppered her feet and legs before travelling upwards. Uncontrollable tremors passed through her when he parted her thighs and settled between them on his knees. Fingers spread the lips at her core open and his tongue flicked at her swollen nub. Sensation swarmed her again. Her hips arched up involuntarily.

"Oh God!" She moaned out loud.

"You're as pink as strawberry ice cream and taste divine."

Using his mouth, he probed, licked, sucked until he had her high on ecstasy. She gripped his head, holding him against her as he expertly took her closer and closer to seventh heaven until she floated over the edge. She tried to hold back, afraid of taking the plunge.

"Let go, Ebony. Come for me," he breathed against her core.

Her womb contracted over and over. And she let go, screaming his name as she soared over the cliffs of total bliss.

When she eventually floated down, she opened her eyes to see Felix beside her, smiling tenderly. He pulled her into his arms, her head on the crook of his arm. She put her hand on his chest and looked up at him, her brain in a fuddle.

Did he just give her pleasure and not expect anything in return? Not believing it, she lifted her head up.

"Felix?"

"Sleep, *ima-mmi*. Tonight was about you. Though I got plenty of pleasure from watching you come apart. Sleep." He kissed her forehead.

Replete and contented, she curled up against him, her eyes drooping into sleep.

Ebony stirred and opened eyes still heavy with sleep. The grey light filtering through the curtains hinted at early dawn. She attempted to shift her position so she could see the table clock on the bedside cabinet and realised she lay trapped. Cocooned against a warm, hard body.

Felix!

She hadn't dreamt it. He had stayed with her in bed all night. More than stayed with her, as she recalled all the sensuous and loving things he did to her body last night. Just thinking of it sent her insides contracting in pleasure. A smile curled her lips and excitement made her heart beat faster.

Her back flush against his chest, his hard arousal lay cradled between her bum cheeks.

He slept naked!

Last night when she fell asleep, he had still been wearing his trousers. When had he removed them?

Wanton need pulsed between her thighs, her body responding instantly. Throwing all caution to the wind, she wriggled her bottom against him. Last night had been wonderful. Still, she remained unfulfilled. Uncompleted. She needed him deep inside so she couldn't tell where she ended and he began.

"Good morning, *ima-mmi*," he whispered in her ear.

His voice, deep and husky, melted her already hot body. His stubble scoured her cheek, sensitising it.

She turned around to face him. He had the sexiest smile she had ever seen. Her heart swelled. This was her man.

"Good morning."

Brushing his lips over hers, he kissed her briefly, his tongue licking the seam from end to end.

"Sleep well?"

His intense dark eyes scanned her face as if he could read her mind. Her cheeks warmed up. Did he know what she wanted him to do to her? What she wanted them to do together?

"Yes, like a baby," she said in a breathy voice. "How's your leg?"

"It's still there." His eyes twinkled with amusement.

"Oh, you! You know what I mean." Playing, she punched his chest.

"I do." His hand caressed her arm, blazing a trail of heat down to her hips.

Filled with courage, she decided to take matters into her own hand. Her husband was always so controlled and in charge; for once, she wanted to be the one to make him come apart.

Moving her hand down his chest, she caressed him. When she flicked the hardened tip of his nipple, a soft sound escaped his lips. Pleasure washed over her at his reaction and she got bolder. She trailed further down until she reached her goal. Wrapping his erection into her palm, she stroked the pulsing, hot and hard steel encased in satin. He groaned and she slid downwards and took the head in her mouth, licking it.

Fingers tangled in her hair and tugged her head back. She stared up at gleaming eyes, his yearning bare and breathtaking. She loved that she could wield this power over him. Loved that he didn't conceal his feelings. For months, she'd thirsted for this type of openness and connection between them.

"Ebony." His voice came out strained and shaky. "You don't have to do this."

"I want to. I want to give you pleasure, too. To return the favour, so to speak."

Thumb stroking her bottom lip, he asked, "Would it give you pleasure?"

"Absolutely," she replied as her core pulsed.

A slight nod of his head and she smiled. That he allowed her this much freedom with his body astounded her. Another side effect of his amnesia and only temporary. She intended to make the most of it.

Leaning down, she fondled his erection, gliding her hand up and down in a slow rhythm. A drop of his pearl aided her action as he hardened and swelled unbelievably in her palm. A flick of her tongue around the head and he let out another groan.

By now, she struggled to control her breathing as her inner thighs slicked with juices. Listening to his pleasure gave her as much delight. Opening her mouth, she took him in and he thrust his hips upwards. Using her hand and her mouth, she worked a steady tempo with Felix's hips canting up and down in tune. She knew he lay close by the low curse he emitted when she put her hand around his balls and squeezed.

"Oh no, you don't," he growled and sat up swiftly, lifting her clear off the bed, ending her attempt to make him lose control using her mouth. He sat her back down astride him, impaling her to the hilt in one carefully manoeuvred movement.

She gasped with pleasure as he expanded inside her and her inner walls gripped him, pulling him further in. He took her lips in an insistent and dominating kiss that brought her close to the edge. Then, gripping her hips, he lifted and slammed her down, knocking the breath out of her as he thrust into her with vigour.

Head tilted back and chest out, she rode him, meeting each thrust with equal gusto. He took her nipple into his mouth, lavishing it with his tongue in between nipping it with his teeth. Sensation surrounded her. Heat travelled in her veins, dragging her closer to rapture.

She clung onto his shoulders as he continued the unrelenting pace. A swipe of his thumb to his tongue then to her swollen nub.

"Give yourself to me," he commanded.

Nothing could hold her back as she soared, screaming his name, wave after wave of orgasm hitting her body, her womb contracting furiously. Then she heard him groan and he expanded within her before he spilled his seed into her womb and joined her in seventh heaven.

Thoroughly sated, Ebony collapsed on top of Felix and he wrapped his arms around her. At last, she was where she belonged. In his arms. In his bed. Nothing else mattered at this moment. Tears pooled in her eyes and dropped onto his chest. He lifted her head up with fingers under her chin and a frown creased his face.

Leaning forward, he kissed the tracks on her cheek. "Don't cry, *ima-mmi*. Did I hurt you?"

She shook her head and smiled weakly. She tried to bury her head back on his chest but he kept it still.

"What's wrong?"

Through teary lashes, she stared at his handsome face. He appeared worried and uncertain. Her macho, all-knowing husband, uncertain. Interesting.

From the first moment she met him, he'd always been confident and sure of himself. Seeing the flicker of worry in his eyes proved how much his lost memories unsettled him. Her heart squeezed in compassion for him, although she sometimes wished they could swap places and she didn't have to live with the horrible memories that plagued her.

"Don't mind me. I'm just so happy. Happy to have you awake again. Happy that you're home at last. Happy that you made loved with me. I feel as if all my birthdays have happened at once. It's silly, isn't it?"

Forehead creased in thought, he watched her for a while before answering.

"It's not silly."

He captured her lips again, a gentle slide of his tongue into her mouth. Needing more, she clung onto his arms and returned the kiss with all the passion she felt for him. He increased the intensity, tilting his head to the side.

With each tangle of their tongues and nip of his teeth, she fell deeper into his snare, all her attention on this man who held her body in his arms. Without doubt, soon her heart would be back in his hands, too.

A tsunami of arousal drenched her just as his erection enlarged and hardened within her. Her insides contracted around it, their bodies reengaging in their sensual dance of love. Hand clasped in her hair, he tipped her head back as his lips peppered her neck, leaving her with tingles that swept her body. The delightful torture continued to her breasts, which he worshipped like a slave, all the while moving slowly within her, his other hand clamped on her hip, controlling their rhythm. He spoke words of endearments in Efik, his breath feathering her skin, making her feverish. Her body temperature climbed with excitement.

How could she not lose her heart to him again when he made love to her as if she was the most priceless possession? When the sensations that burned through her invited him to possess her completely and wipe away all the bad memories?

Ima-mmi. He used the loving term every day since he awoke from coma. She wanted to believe he loved her. That she was his one and only true love.

Right now, he treated her as if he truly meant it, encouraging her to show him how she felt, too. Her hands roamed his taut flesh, her fingers playing with his nipples, eliciting a deep groan of pleasure from him. She explored his body and thrilled at its perfection; toned muscles showed his weeks in hospital had only made him leaner without any flab in sight.

Her lips tasted his skin, his saltiness, his essence. Licking him. Nipping him.

"You are so sweet, so beautiful." He ground into her. "And you're all mine."

His declaration had her already racing heart tripping over itself. Then his lips claimed hers, his tongue mirroring the actions of his hard, enlarged rod within her. Her orgasm took her unawares and she screamed his name into his mouth. He followed her soon afterwards and the two of them crashed back onto the bed.

They both curled up together, his body cocooning her. Contented, she allowed her smile to show. For the first time in months, her soul found peace and joy.

"*Ima-mmi*, tell me how I proposed to you?" his voice deep and irresistible.

Still, her body tensed.

"I understand if you don't want to talk about it, but it would really make me happy if you would tell me." He spoke so close to her ear, sensitising her skin with goose bumps.

Letting out a deep sigh, she said, "It's all right. I want to tell you."

His arms tightened around her body and she relaxed once again and recalled the event.

Five months earlier

"Hello, Ebony."

At hearing her name, Ebony glanced up and her heart rate picked up with alarm.

Felix's tall, athletic frame loomed large above her. He looked appealing in his crisp white shirt and navy blue trousers. His shirt had the top three buttons undone, showing off the dark V of his neck and chest; the sleeves rolled up, revealing well-toned lower arms dusted with short dark hairs. His wide smile softened the harsh angles of his warrior's face and his midnight eyes sparkled.

"Hi, Felix," she replied, a touch out of breath, and stood up as he came towards her.

He leaned forward and kissed her on both cheeks. She caught a scent of his spicy aftershave, reminding her of the day he'd picked her from the airport. Without thinking, she inhaled deeply. When he stepped back, she avoided his eyes for a brief moment as heat travelled up her body at her shameless reaction.

"It's nice to see you again."

Lowering her lashes, she glanced at him through their dark veil and noticed him watching her without flinching. Their gazes connected, his black eyes now with flecks of crimson, turning her already heated blood into lava. For a moment, she forgot her location, everything else but the two of them. Until she heard a cough and the brief enchantment broke as she realised her friend tried to get her attention.

"It is nice to see you again, Felix.... This is my friend, Faith." Ebony recovered her composure enough to give an innocent smile to her friend who, in turn, had the I-want-to-know-what's-going-on-here look. She would have to do some explaining later.

"Hi, Faith. It's nice to meet you." Felix flashed a charming smile.

"Likewise," Faith replied, stretching out her hand to shake his, which he shook briefly before turning back to face Ebony.

"I'm here with my brother. Would you like to join us?" He nodded in the direction he'd come from.

Ebony looked enquiringly at her friend, who gave her a knowing look and shrugged. Faith should be shocked that Ebony became the one "picking" up men, or rather, being "picked" up by a man, considering her history.

"Sure. Why not? The more the merrier, right?" she replied to Felix.

He led them upstairs into an exclusive section of the lounge. A tall, dark, good-looking man who could have been a spitting image of Felix except for their skin tones sat there. Felix being darker, still, there would be no mistaking the fact they were brothers. The man rose from his seat as they approached.

"Mark. Fancy meeting you here," Faith chirped.

"Faith, it's nice to see you again." Mark had a lazy smile on his face as he kissed Faith on both cheeks. He seemed to have an easy-going personality and charm.

"You two know each other?" Felix asked with a mix of surprise and humour, his dark brow arching upwards.

"You could say that. We met at a finance conference in South Africa two weeks ago. And this must be Ebony," Mark said, smoothly turning to Ebony. "It's great to finally meet you. I've heard so much about you." He gave a mischievous wink at Felix, who, in turn, glared at him.

"Really?" Ebony amused herself by watching the brothers. So easy to see that whilst Felix had the reserved charm, Mark turned out the out-going player. Their interaction made her wonder what her relationship would have been with her brother if he'd been around still. Feeling a dark cloud descend on her, she shook her head, turning her attention back to Felix.

"Mark, I warn you. I'll wring your neck if you say another word." Felix glowered and his brother simply laughed in response.

"Don't mind Mark. He's just playing the fool. Please sit down," he said to Ebony, before turning another withering look at Mark who kept chuckling, his attention now on Faith.

The men waited for the ladies to sit down, Mark next to Faith and Felix next to Ebony.

Cosy.

Ebony saw Faith give her the same knowing look again and she smiled to herself.

Faith, her sassy, outgoing, independent, girl-power friend, had dragged her out tonight because she had been complaining about being bored and missing her life in the States.

Since her arrival in Lagos over a week ago, she hadn't done much except deal with the throng of visitors arriving in their family home in preparation for the ten-year memorial service for her father and brother. The only respite she'd had came by logging on to Facebook and reconnecting with her friends online.

Back in the States, she had worked as an analyst for the World Trade Organisation. As the ten-year anniversary of the tragic accident that claimed the lives of her brother and father approached, she had requested a year out of work. She needed the break and the time to reacquaint herself with her fatherland.

Also, her mum had been appointed to run a non-governmental organisation to deal with International Trade in Nigeria, and she wanted Ebony to help with setting it up. Ebony had been enthusiastic about getting involved in the project, but there wasn't much for her to do at the moment. She learned things went at a different, much slower pace out here. So for now, here she found herself, free and listless and going out of her mind because she needed to keep busy all the time. Being idle gave her too much thinking time. Time to think about people who shouldn't be on her radar.

Like the man sitting next to her, for one.

Ten days since she saw him last, but she'd thought about him several times every one of those days. She should know better. Dele Savage, her ex-fiancé, had ensured she didn't want anything to do with any man again.

This encounter with Felix would only be a drink and a chat. *Nothing more*, she told herself.

Lifting his hand, Felix called the waiter over and ordered their drinks. After the waiter left with their orders, he turned to Ebony.

"So, how is your mother?" he asked her as he leaned back into the sofa and stretched his legs in front of him.

The motion drew her attention to his powerful thighs. She remembered the hardness when she'd touched him in the car, and her pulse picked up speed.

"She's fine. Our house has been busy with visitors for the past week. I'd forgotten how chaotic it can get." Talking helped to distract her from Felix's raw masculinity. She needed to get a grip.

"What about you? How are you coping?"

He said that so low, his voice so husky, it felt as if he'd breathed it over her neck. Her skin tingled. Vibrations pitted in her belly, massaging her insides. It took her a while to find her voice. She had to clear the lump in it by coughing.

"Me.... Oh, I'm doing great," she said, waving her hand in a dismissive gesture and casting a furtive glance at her friend. Deep in conversation with Mark, Faith seemed oblivious to Ebony and Felix.

They're getting on well. A bit too well.

"Is that so?" Felix asked.

She turned back to face him. His dark brow raised an inch and his cheek dimpled as his smile deepened.

"Remember, it's me. You can tell me how it is, the plain truth, not the sugar-coated version." He put his hand on her arm and his heat permeated her skin.

What was it about Felix? She'd only met him twice, yet, there seemed to be a rapport, a connection, that ran deeper that any she could remember. She could talk to him, which felt strange because she found it difficult talking to anyone else. Even Faith didn't know her darkest thoughts. But it seemed Felix could sense them.

"You want the unvarnished truth?" She closed her eyes, trying to banish her thoughts, but something in his voice when he spoke again caused her to open them.

"Nothing but," he replied. "It never pays to coat the truth. It does come out, eventually—with devastating consequences."

His eyes darkened and she caught a brief glimpse of a troubled soul.

What would have caused him such pain? Suddenly wanting to soothe his pain, she touched his thigh to reassure him. He looked down at her hand on his leg. When he raised his gaze back up at her face, the darkness had gone from him. He smiled again and pulled her hand up to brush her knuckles with a kiss. For a moment, she forgot her thoughts and just stared at his lips on her tingling hand.

"Come on. Let's hear it. You're not trying to avoid answering my question, are you?" he teased.

His amused black eyes sparkled like diamonds, his tone playful when he released her hand. Absentmindedly, she rubbed the spot he'd kissed.

"Of course not." She feigned indignation. "The truth is I miss my old life, my friends. I'm bored. The project I'm going to work doesn't start for another week or so. And Mum wants me to travel to our hometown with her although she hasn't said when yet. I've got mixed feelings about that, too.... I don't know. I just can't wait to start my new job so I don't go stir-crazy."

"I think you need to see more of Nigeria. There is so much to do. Tell you what." He gave a wide and enticing smile. "Why don't you come down to the East with me for a few days? I have to go to Port Harcourt for a meeting on

Friday. I have a villa in Calabar. We can make a weekend of it. How about that?"

"It sounds great. I'd love to do some travelling but...I don't think it is a good idea to go with you."

As bad ideas go, spending the weekend alone with Felix counted as one so soon after Dele. Her past experience proved she didn't know how to have a casual fling. One hundred percent or nothing. Her physical reaction to Felix showed she was en route to all with a man who had a reputation for flings.

His lips moved in a smile filled with seductive intent. "If it will make you feel any better, you can invite your friend along." He turned to look at his brother chatting intensely with Faith. "I'm sure Mark wouldn't mind coming along since they seem to be getting on so well over there."

"Someone's talking about me," Mark interjected as he turned to face them. "What's going on?"

"I was just saying maybe the four of us should go down to Calabar for the weekend. What do you think?"

"No can do, bro. I've already got plans for the weekend."

"Sorry. Neither can I. Some other time, maybe," Faith added.

Felix turned back to Ebony. "Oh, well. I did try. If you do change your mind, let me know. In the meantime, though, dance with me." He stood up and held out his hand.

Ebony stared at his hand with wary reluctance. This thing between them moved at a pace faster than she wanted to go. Felix proved too good-looking, charming, and so easy to get along with.

Do I want to get involved with him?

He hadn't asked her out. Yet.

If we carry on like this, I will fall for him. I know this with the same confidence I know the sun will rise tomorrow.

She sucked in a deep breath.

No men. No dating. For now, I have my career, my friends, and my mum to concentrate on.

Felix, probably sensing her hesitation, leaned closer and whispered in her ear, his breath feathering her neck, sensitising it. "It's only a dance, *ima-mmi*. I promise I won't bite."

Heat travelled through her and she looked up sharply, her eyes connecting with his fiery ones and her heart rate increased. Unable to stop herself, she took his hand and let him pull her up. "African Queen" by Tuface Idibia played from the hidden speakers behind the dark walls. It used to be one of her favourite songs but each time she heard it, it reminded her of Dele singing it to her.

Felix pulled her closer when they got to the small dance floor. She put her arms around him, revelling in the firm heat of his body. When the words of the music hit her, she stiffened.

"Listen, Felix, I like you but I can't do this—" she stopped, not sure if she wanted to go down this route of speech.

"What can't you do, Ebony?"

The way Felix watched her with intent, he must've seen the troubles in her eyes. He frowned. When she pulled back, he let her go.

"Okay, let's sit down and you can tell me what's wrong."

She nodded. He put his hand on her back as they walked to the sofa. Mark and Faith were nowhere to be seen.

When they sat down, Ebony avoided his gaze, picking up her drink. She didn't sip from it but stared into the light liquid, her face creased in a frown, instead.

"I...I can't get into a relationship right now. I recently broke up with my fiancé. He called off our wedding a month before the date. I...I just want to focus on my career for now."

"What happened?"

The gentle way he asked almost made her cry.

"I don't want to talk about it." She turned away from him, picking at non-existent fluff on her dress.

"You still love him."

She looked up at him as she relived the hurt.

"I was in love with him for a very long time. It's not that easy to just switch it off after a relationship is over."

"He is a fool for letting you go. But I think I have a solution to your heartache."

"You do? What is it?"

"Marry me."

"Really? I proposed to you just weeks after meeting you?" Felix had a big grin on his face as he turned her around to face him in the bed.

"Yes, it was more like days but who's counting." She giggled and then yawned, their intense lovemaking taking its toll.

"I must have been madly in love with you."

Her smile disappeared and she averted her eyes. *Tell him the rest.* Her conscience pricked her.

"Something like that." She said instead. She wasn't telling lies, just omitting things.

Warm hands massaged her back, lulling her into a sleepy state.

"I'm glad you're finally Mrs. Felix Essien in the true sense." She heard his satisfied whisper as she drifted off.

The next time Ebony woke, the aroma of rich, freshly filtered, ground coffee drifted into her nostrils. She lifted her head and stretched with languor. Felix was not in bed with her. The sun must be high up in the sky, given the light that flooded the bedroom. Her eyes followed the smell of the coffee to the low table by the settee. A tray laden with food sat there. Swinging legs over the side, she got up and grabbed her silk robe now laid out at the foot of the bed. She put it on and cinched the sash around her waist.

Felix strode out of the walk-in wardrobe, the cane he leaned on for support tapping on the slate flooring. Despite his obvious injury, he still carried an aura of charm, confidence, and carnality. He wore a new pair of dark brown cargo trousers and a white linen shirt, the buttons on them undone. Eyes riveted to his chest and abs, her heart rate picked up and she wondered how she could still want him so soon after this morning's lovemaking session. She had felt sated at the time. Yet, as she stood mesmerised, she yearned for him all over again.

"Sleeping Beauty wakes." His low voice sounded decadent and vibrated through her. Her sex clenched and she tugged her bottom lip with her teeth.

Ten years in a relationship and I can't remember ever being this insatiable. One day with Felix and I don't want to leave the bedroom.

Lady of the House was at risk of being run over by Sex Bomb this morning.

One minute she contemplated falling to her knees and begging him to take her back to bed. The next, one hand wrapped the side of her face and he said, "When you do that with your lip, I can't resist kissing it."

And he gave her a thorough, breath-stealing kiss.

Felix gripped his walking cane tight, just as his desire for Ebony flared again. His fingers tangled with the curls of her hair. It seemed she looked her sexiest first thing in the morning with her hair wild, messy, and fiery. She leaned into him, pressing warm hands on his chest just above nipples that seemed to harden anytime she touched him. Pulse rate increasing, he bit back a groan and pulled back.

"I think you better get something to eat before I haul you back into that bed." He curled his lips and grinned with appreciation.

Her chin dipped and she lowered her gaze in a timid smile. He chuckled. How could she be so shy after what she did to him with her tongue this morning? Just thinking about it made his trousers suddenly too tight. He wanted a repeat performance. Fingers still in her hair, he gave a gentle tug and until she looked up at him. Amber eyes sparkled with sensual invitation.

He let out a groan and released her. Right here and right now, he was happy.

"You shouldn't have let me sleep for so long," she said as she swept past him and settled on the gold and brown, brocade-covered Victorian-style settee, feet crossed at ankles and tucked to the side. A ladylike pose, yet the silk robe stopped mid-thigh, showing off her legs. "I was hoping to sort out breakfast for you but you beat me to it."

Pictures of Ebony sitting legs braced either side of him played out in his mind and he barely registered her words.

"Felix?" Her curved brow quirked in a bemused smile.

Snapping out of his trance, he shrugged and lowered his body beside her. "I just told Bisi what to prepare and hey, presto." He waved his hand at the table.

There was a jug of freshly squeezed orange juice, a cafetière of fresh coffee, sliced melon crescents, omelette, and toasted bread. He poured a glass of juice and handed it to her.

Ebony sipped the juice. "I'm not sure I can eat all this. Maybe just some toast."

He shook his head. "You have to eat. I can't have you wilting away. What will your mother think?"

Head whipped back, she gazed at him wide-eyed.

"You remember Mum?" she asked and gave him a beautiful smile. "That's great. Your memory is coming back. What else do you remember?"

Her palm wrapped around his lower arm, fingers caressing him.

The image of the elegant, dark-skinned, wheelchair-bound woman swam into his mind. But how did he do that?

He squeezed his brain, trying to remember more. But the memory proved fleeting and gone, his mind in a fog again. He shook his head in frustration.

"This is good. It means that soon, it'll all come back." She hugged him tight.

Inhaling a deep breath, he allowed the excitement in her voice to soothe his annoyance.

"Yes, you're right. I'm sure it'll happen soon. I'm in the right place." He paused, hoping the rest would come to him quickly. Living with chunks of his memory blank remained totally frustrating. "So eat up. I don't want Mrs. Duru giving me a hard time about not taking better care of you."

He spread some honey on a slice of toast and held it up for her to bite into. As she did, a drop smeared her chin. Without thinking, he leaned forward and swiped the runny sweet with his tongue. He heard the hitch in her breath, and the pulse on the base of her neck jumped quickly. She'd made a similar sound last night when he'd swiped his tongue against her clit. Her eager response nearly undid him.

Heart racing, he fought to maintain control.

He took a fork and picked up some omelette.

"Open up."

She eyed the omelette before parting her lips, eyes trained on him. Pink tongue flicked out and he placed the food in her mouth.

Rock hard, he shifted in his seat. His intention had been to show her so much decadent pleasure and hopefully wipe out his previous sins against her. Now, he ran the risk of blue balls syndrome.

At this rate, she wouldn't be finishing her breakfast. Even after their early morning bout of lovemaking, this had taken him to total bliss and beyond. He wanted to haul her back into bed and start all over again.

No. She needed nourishment. Last night, she hadn't eaten dinner. She didn't exactly look unwell but something didn't seem right. At the thought, his heart pounded into his chest. Surely, she couldn't be unwell. Maybe he should ask their family doctor to look her over.

He carried on feeding her and watched as she chewed each piece, every slide of her tongue against her lips and gulp as she swallowed fuelled his aching granite erection.

"You know now you've started this, you'll have to keep it up." She beamed a teasing smile at him.

"I intend to keep spoiling you. You deserve it." He wiped some crumbs off her chin with a napkin.

"I hope we are like this always." The melancholy in her voice clicked a warning in his mind. Her eyes lost their sparkle.

"There's no reason why it should be any different, is there?" he asked and issued a silent prayer.

"I'm just saying 'cause sometimes, things change. People change. Nothing lasts forever." She looked away.

The tightening in his chest made it difficult to breath. He couldn't allow whatever had happened in the past to ruin this beautiful moment. Fingers gripping her chin, he applied pressured until she turned her head and met his gaze.

"Why are we worrying about forever when we have right here and right now? Sure, I want this feeling to last." He drew in a steadying breath. "But just as I don't want to worry about the past that I don't remember, I have no intention of worrying about a future I can't foresee. We need to take it one day at a time. Live for the moment. Are you with me?"

"I...I don't know," she muttered.

Her hesitation wrenched at his guts, a lancing poker on an open sore, the first time since the day she'd agreed in hospital to give their marriage a chance. Now the past threatened to dampen their bliss. He wouldn't give up without a fight.

"Ebony, are you with me? In this journey, you are either with me or not. It's a yes or a no. But you have to be completely honest. What's it going to be?"

"Yes." This time, she appeared more emphatic with her response.

Relief washed over him. He exhaled a deep breath he hadn't realised he held and gathered her in his arms, forehead to forehead, eyes closed.

For a brief moment, he'd thought the joy had come to an end. More than anything else, the thought of losing his wife scared him. An irrational fear, considering he'd only known her for a little over a week, of what he could remember, anyhow.

And yet, a frown creased his brows. He needed to find out what went wrong between them and hoped Ebony would trust him enough to tell him herself. If she didn't, he'd have to find another way.

"What do you want to do today?" he asked her when he leaned back, changing the subject.

"I hadn't thought that far ahead. Just whatever you want to do."

"Okay. How about you get dressed and I make a few calls. Then we can go out, to the beach. A day at the beach. Sun, sea, and sand. We can have a picnic, too. How's that?"

She looked at his leg with uncertainty. "What about all that sand and your cast?"

"Leave that to me. Just worry about organising the picnic. The sea air will be good for us after those weeks in hospital."

A smile lit up her face. "Sounds great. I'll sort out the picnic. You go do whatever you need to do."

He tugged her into his arms one last time, kissing her long and hard and letting her scent permeate his pores. When he released her, they were both panting hard.

Instead of carrying her back onto the bed as his body demanded, he picked up the cane and headed for the door, his missing memories uppermost on his mind. He turned just in time to see Ebony get up, walk into the bathroom, and shut the door. Something bugged his wife and he needed to know what. High time he spoke to Mark.

CHAPTER SIX

Ebony stepped into the bathroom, overcome by a rolling wave of nausea, and rushed to the bowl to retch. It racked her body. She held on tight to stop herself from keeling over, her body weakened. When the ebb subsided, she sat on the cold tiles, relieved as they cooled her hot skin. Eventually, she clutched the edge of the sink and stood up after the queasiness subsided.

This could no longer be a stomach bug. It had gone on for too long. She racked her brain for what could be wrong with her.

It hit her. *Oh, God!* Hands griping the sink, her body swayed.

Period way overdue, she did the mental calculation. Had to be at least eight weeks late. At first, she'd put the lateness down to stress. Irregular periods occurred with her, partly why she got prescribed the pill.

And that was the other thing. She was on the pill, so she couldn't be pregnant, could she?

Pregnant? God help her.

The prospect of a baby would change the dynamics of her relationship with Felix. A certainty. He'd been adamant about this one thing before they'd gotten married. She should've known their interlude in nirvana wouldn't last long.

Sure, he seemed delirious about having her around. His desire for her would all change when he found out she got pregnant. *If* she'd gotten pregnant. Another wave of nausea hit her and she emptied out whatever remained from last night.

When she stood up again, she stepped into the massive shower enclosure and turned on the warm spray. She had to find out for herself and decide what to do before Felix discovered this. After showering, she got dressed and went downstairs to find her husband. She had to go out to buy the kit for the pregnancy test.

She found him in his office reading a newspaper, injured leg on a small upholstered foot rest. Reclining in an oxblood leather wingback armchair and with sleeves rolled up baring chocolate arms wrapped in sinewy muscles, he was a billboard for pure casual masculinity. An invitation for her to climb onto his lap. A shiver of pleasure ran down her spine.

Ignoring the naughty thought and the two leather armchairs facing his dark wood desk, she stood by the door.

"I need to go out quickly. I forgot I needed to get some stuff."

"I sent Patrick on a quick errand with the Cayenne," he said, glancing up from the paper. "I just wanted to make sure it was ready for our trip this afternoon. Let me call Kola to drive you." He reached for the desk phone.

"No." The reply came out sharper than she'd wanted and by the way his dark brow rose almost to his hairline, he noticed.

"There's no need," she continued to cover up her anxiety. "I can take one of the other cars and drive myself. I won't be long."

The words came out in a rush. The thought of being pregnant threatened to unhinge her. Oh, she would love to have a child. But this one spelled disaster for her blossoming marriage.

"Okay." If he suspected anything, he didn't show it.

"See you later." Puffing out a relieved breath, she turned to leave.

"Hey. Don't I get a kiss?" His voice rumbled behind her. Wood scraped against stone.

Not wanting him to know anything could be wrong, she clutched trembling hands to her midriff, walked to him, and sat on his lap. She lifted her face up to give him a brief kiss.

Hands wrapped either side of her head, he took over, greedy lips and tongue ravaging her mouth. She sighed and relaxed into him, hunger for him replacing worries.

"You better hurry." Lips trailed the sensitive skin behind her left ear. "Otherwise, I'll come looking for you." Fingers brushed curly strands off her face, black eyes sucking her into a black hole of craving. "I've got plans for us this afternoon."

She swallowed, working her heavy tongue.

"I won't be long." She sounded breathless and her knees trembled as she stood.

"Sure. I'll see you when you get back." Letting her go, he swatted her bottom playfully.

As soon as oak door shut behind Ebony, Felix picked up the cordless telephone and pressed the button to call Kola.

"Yes, bro." The instant response.

"Ebony is going out. I want someone to follow her and find out where she's going," he spoke without preamble.

"Patrick should be back any minute," Kola replied. "If not, I'll take her."

"No. She doesn't want a driver. She's going by herself."

"She is?" Kola's reply echoed Felix's reaction when Ebony refused to be driven.

She hid something from him. He sensed it when she walked into his office. She had tried to hide it but he knew something wasn't right. Her body had been tense under his touch and she'd avoided his gaze. Her sudden need to go out shopping when earlier she'd said she hadn't planned to do anything also made him suspicious. She'd even hesitated about kissing him just now. An almost imperceptible hesitation, but he'd noticed. She couldn't still be shy about physical contact with him after all they'd done last night and this morning. Alarm bells went off loudly in his head. He knew better than to ignore them.

"That's what she said," Felix said in a hard tone.

"No *wahala*. I'll follow her in the Range."

Ordinarily, he should have implicit trust in his wife. Yet, there were so many unanswered questions about her, him, and their marriage. She knew what happened on their wedding night; she'd been there with him. Yet, she remained unwilling to tell him. He couldn't shake off the look in her eyes, or the words she spoke sometimes, like this morning when he'd asked her if she was with him and she'd replied that she didn't know. That had upset him but he had chosen to ignore it at the time. What it made clear to him was that she had doubts about their marriage. Doubts he didn't understand but intended to, soon enough.

"No. I don't want her to know she is being followed."

"Okay. Freddy can do it using one of the smaller cars." If Kola thought his request was strange, he didn't indicate it in his voice, discretion being a major part of security. "Hold on a minute."

Felix heard Kola issuing instructions to another man, presumably Freddy, who replied "Yes, boss" before Kola came back on the line.

"Ebony just drove out and Freddy is following behind," Kola said.

"Good."

If he'd done something wrong to Ebony, then he needed to make things right. However, he couldn't do that if he didn't know what he went up against. He had promised her he would be a good husband and he intended to follow through.

What if *she* had done something wrong? That might explain why she hid things from him. Yet, he couldn't believe that she would. The devoted, loving Ebony he knew would never do anything to hurt him, would she? Pain twisted his insides like someone had stuck a knife in his gut, and he gripped the edges of his chair.

He would be a fool not to find out the truth sooner rather than later. His mother had left it too late to find out about his father's infidelity and had paid the ultimate price. He wouldn't undergo the same fate. But better off not thinking about it until he found out the truth for himself.

"Whilst I was in hospital, you drove her everywhere, right?" Felix asked, tapping his fingertips on the wooden desk top.

"Yes, either I or one of the other guys did," Kola replied.

"I want a report of everywhere she went during that period."

"I can tell you now. The only places she visited outside the hospital and home were her mother's house and the shopping mall."

"Are you certain?" Felix frowned.

"Yes. The team always provided an update at the end of each day."

"Thank you. That'll be all." He hung up. Kola being the best at what he did, he trusted his words. They should have made Felix happy, but no. He still had too many unanswered questions.

After Ebony picked up the pregnancy kit from the pharmacy, she sat in the car in the shopping mall car park debating what to do next. She didn't want to take the kit home and do the test there. Felix would likely see the result before she prepared herself to tell him. She could go to her mother's, but her mother would have too many questions she wasn't ready to answer right now. She picked up her phone from her bag and called Faith. It rang, then her friend picked up.

"Girl, you remember me today." Faith's chirpy voice resounded in her ear.

"Are you home?" She had to get straight to the point; otherwise, she'd lose her nerve. Moreover, her time lay short.

"Yes. Is everything okay?" Her friend toned her voice down with concern.

"I'm coming over. I'll explain when I get there."

"Okay. See you soon."

Ebony put her phone back in her bag and started the car ignition to drive to Faith's waterside apartment in the Lekki peninsula. When she got there and Faith opened the door, she didn't wait for the other woman to say anything.

"I need to use your bathroom."

Faith looked puzzled but waved her on. "Sure. You know where it is."

Ebony walked into the bathroom and shut the door behind her. Taking out the test kit from her bag, she carried out the instructions. She left the kit on the counter and washed her hands before stepping out.

Faith stood in her living room, watching her with a curious expression.

"Ebony, I know that look on your face. What's the matter?"

Ebony exhaled a deep breath, hoping to loosen the tension in her stomach. It didn't help. She bit her lip, her arms wrapped around her waist. "I might be pregnant. Well, I'll find out for sure in about three minutes." She glanced at her watch, the knot in her belly tightening with anxiety.

"Wow, congratulations!" Faith said, moving towards her but stopped mid-step. "But I take it from your expression that it's not good news. Why?" She folded her arms across her chest, her confusion obvious on her pretty face.

"Faith, I'm sorry I deceived you."

"What the hell are you talking about?"

Ebony paced the room, unable to quell her agitation.

"My marriage to Felix is not real."

"Not real. Are you on medication or something? Have you forgotten I was there as your maid of honour? I watched you take the vows and sign the certificates."

"I know. I know. That's not what I meant." She sighed. "Let me explain. Remember the day we went out together right after I'd just arrived in Nigeria?"

Faith frowned.

"Come on, it was the day we met both Felix and his brother Mark at the bar."

"Oh, yes. I remember now."

Five months earlier, on the night Felix proposed to Ebony.

Marry her?

Shock would be an understatement as far as Ebony was concerned. Her ears must have played up. She had to pick her open mouth up off the floor.

"I'm sorry, but I don't think I heard you correctly. Did you just tell me to marry you?"

He hadn't asked, just stated the words in a casual tone. Like saying the sun would set tonight. A certainty.

She stared up into Felix's face, looking for signs of drunkenness. He looked sober, his midnight eyes clear, expression serious. Deadly serious.

"Yes, I did." His response struck her as emphatic, his stare unwavering. "It would solve your problem as well as mine."

"Are you out of your mind? I just told you I don't want to get involved in another relationship. How is getting married to you not a relationship?" Ebony's agitation drove her to wave her hands in the air.

Felix raised his hand in a placating manner.

"Just hear me out first." His tone remained calm and serious.

Ebony glared at him, backing away a touch. She'd moved so close to him in her confrontation, their faces only inches apart, his warm breath fanning her cheek.

"Okay. I'm listening."

"I've got a problem. The board of directors for the Apex Group of Companies wants me to get married. They've issued an ultimatum and a date by which I have to tie the knot, or they vote to oust me from my position as Managing Director. I personally don't want to get married. Don't ask me why." He paused, eyes intent as if studying her response.

Ebony maintained an outward appearance of passivity, though her heart still raced with tension and disbelief.

"However, I realise I have to appease the board, albeit temporarily, until I can acquire a stronger base. What I need is a suitable lady to play the role. We'll get married before the deadline date and live to all purposes as man and wife. I'll pay her a specified amount at the end of the marriage. While we are married, she'll have access to everything the wife of the head of a major private bank should have access to. At the end of the two year period, we get divorced and she walks away with her settlement and all that she acquired whilst married to me."

Ebony had never heard anything so ridiculous. She'd heard of arranged marriages. But marriage as a business arrangement? No way!

What was wrong with him? Why would a young, rich, handsome, and virile man like Felix want to pay someone to marry him? He had to be pulling her leg.

"So how do I fit into your well laid-out plans? You can marry any woman you want. In fact, I know plenty who would kill to get their hands on you." She swept her gaze up and down his body as she spoke sarcastically.

"Those are the women that I want to avoid—the ones who'll become emotionally involved and demand more when I am unable to provide. You, on the other hand, have stated quite equivocally that you don't want to get involved, which means you have no intentions of being emotionally attached to any man. Right?" He paused, watching her closely. He cocked his head to one side, waiting for her response.

The tension in her stomach tightened under his scrutiny.

"Yes...." she said, suddenly unsure of where he was going with this. She wasn't some cold-blooded bitch that could marry a man and not be emotionally involved with him.

"Well, that suits me very well." He shrugged. "You spoke about your recent split from your fiancé. I can only imagine the social headache that must've caused you and your mother, especially having to cancel so close to a wedding date.... How about getting back at the man who broke your heart by showing him you got over him in record time? I'm sure your mother will be very happy to see you settle down."

He had a valid point. A part of her wanted to get back at Dele—to show him that she'd moved on. That she had done better than him. Felix represented a great catch. More man than Dele, judging by their encounters so far. But something still didn't sit well with her.

"Yes, my mother will be very pleased to see me get married." A blanket of sadness wrapped around her whenever she thought about her mother. What Ebony wouldn't give to see her mother filled with joy and laughter again. "Still, what happens when the marriage breaks up? She'll certainly be upset, then. How are we going to explain that?" she replied with a boldness she didn't feel at that moment.

"Marriages break up so easily these days. We could simply tell her it hasn't worked out between us. She can't hold that against us."

Felix sounded so certain but Ebony just couldn't shake the feeling that this would be wrong. She didn't want to deceive her mother even if the act of getting married would make her happy. Yet, deep within her, the urge to help Felix weighed her down. There had to be another way.

"So when do you have to get married by?" she asked in a sedate tone, trying to rack her brain for an alternative solution.

"First of January."

Her eyes almost popped out. "That's less than two months away. It's not enough time to plan a wedding. No, I can't do it," she blurted out while shaking her head. This whole thing reeked of crazy disaster, anyway.

"Yes, it's not enough time if we were planning a big wedding with bells and whistles attached. But this is just for show. If we keep it to the barest minimum, and the guest list to family and friends, then we should be able to do it. Moreover, I think my brother, Tony's, current girlfriend is a wedding planner, so we could probably use her services to make things easier," Felix stated in a matter-of-fact tone, as if he were discussing some business transaction.

His calm appearance and cool concentration unnerved her. She looked away, trying not to get distracted by his intense gaze.

"That's handy."

Whenever worried, she chewed her bottom lip, like now. Another thought entered her head. She spoke it out loud before she had processed the implications.

"What about children?"

"No children. This is going to be a temporary arrangement so there is no need to bring children into it to suffer when we split up." He sounded so emphatic, so sure that it left Ebony feeling disconcerted but she wasn't sure why.

"Oh...okay," she spluttered, suddenly thrown off balance when the image of her holding a chubby baby boy with Felix's dark eyes sprang into her mind.

Butterflies fluttered low inside her. If he didn't want children, did that mean there would be no intimacy, no passion, and no lovemaking? She looked at Felix's all too masculine body again. What a shame. A big fat travesty. A warm shiver washed over her body. If she married Felix, she would want to spend every night in his arms and in his bed. Nowhere else. His presence lit a spark within her that threatened to raze her, to turn her into puddle of need. It would only get worse if she married him.

Except she didn't want to marry him, did she?

"Listen. Think about it. You don't have to give me an answer tonight. I know you need to process the information and decide if it's the right thing for you. You can give me your answer tomorrow night when I pick you up for dinner." His lips widened in a smile, dimpling his cheeks, and his dark eyes twinkled like stars.

She nodded, relieved that she didn't have to give an answer straight away. She smiled cheekily when the full meaning of his words filtered to her brain. "Nice one, but your distraction tactics failed. I don't remember agreeing to a dinner date. Why don't I just tell you my answer on the phone?"

"Because I enjoy your company so much that I'm sure you wouldn't deprive a desperate man of it, would you?"

Before she could respond with a nifty retort, her phone beeped in her purse and she picked it up. A text message from Faith.

We've gone to get some Suya. You were enjoying yourself so much I didn't want to disturb you. You can come join us, if you like. xoxo F.

Trust Faith and her matchmaking antics. Ebony smiled and shook her head.

"That was Faith. Mark's taken her to get some *suya*. We're invited, if we like. I think that's another way of her saying 'don't you dare disturb us'." Ebony laughed.

"I think so, too. They barely gave us a moment's notice whilst they were here." Felix laughed, too, his husky tone threatening to melt her bones.

"Not that we gave them a moment's notice, either. Now I feel guilty because we were supposed to be out together." She started chewing her lower lip again.

"Hey, stop doing that. You are in danger of damaging your lovely lips."

Smiling, Felix reached across and tilted Ebony's face upwards with his fingers, caressing her lower lip gently with his thumb, as if soothing out the damage her teeth had caused.

"Next time you chew your lip, I'll have to kiss it better."

Heart skipping a beat, her breath hitched in her throat and warmth spread all over her. With her lips tingling at his

103

touch, she couldn't say a word. Just sat mesmerised under his starry gaze, wishing he would carry out his threat.

Instead, Felix leaned back and dropped his hand. "Let me take you home."

Nodding, Ebony couldn't shake the curious mix of disappointment and relief that descended on her. She picked up her purse and walked out of the bar with Felix's arm around her shoulder.

CHAPTER SEVEN

Ebony remained on edge for a couple of days. Felix had called her two days earlier to cancel their dinner date. He'd had to travel to Johannesburg on urgent business and wasn't due back in Lagos until today.

This afternoon, she strolled through the detailed, sizeable garden at the back of her parent's modest, colonial-style home. But her thoughts focused less on the beautiful variety of plants, layers, and colours displayed by the different trees, shrubs, and flowers. The main thing on her mind became Felix and his bizarre marriage proposal.

His giving her breathing space to make up her mind should have cheered her. Strangely, it didn't. She wanted to hear his voice and his reassurance that whatever decision she made would be the right one.

Why she needed that level of validation from him, she couldn't decipher. She'd been independent since eighteen and had been able to make decisions about her life without input from others in the past.

So why was this one different?

When she bit her lower lip in her usual manner—a sure sign she worried about something—she realised what her action meant and stopped.

Ebony noticed their housekeeper walking towards her. Margaret—a slim, middle-aged lady—had worked for them for as long as Ebony could remember. She got up from the bench and met the woman in the middle of the curvilinear cobbled path carved in the otherwise green lawn. When Margaret told Ebony her mother wanted to see her, she followed the housekeeper indoors. Her mother waited in the ground floor sitting room.

"Mum, you wanted to see me?" Ebony said when she walked into the spacious room filled with sturdy, antique African furniture and family ornaments. On the off-white walls hung a mixture of family portraits and paintings from well-known African artists. Her mother sat on a mink-coloured upholstered sofa, one of the few modern items in the room.

"Yes, come and have a look. A bouquet of flowers just arrived. Aren't they just lovely? Begonias, African tulips, and chrysanthemums—some of my favourites." Her mother waved in the direction of the flowers set in a white porcelain vase on the mahogany sideboard.

"They are beautiful. Who sent them?" Ebony asked as she walked over to take a closer look.

"I don't know. Margaret just brought them in but I think there is a card attached."

"There is," Ebony said as she stood in front of the bouquet, inhaling its sweet, exotic fragrance. Reluctant to pick up the card, her hand hovered above as she stood unsure who might have sent it.

"Go on. Read the card and end our misery." Her mother encouraged her with a smile as if sensing Ebony's hesitation.

Ebony picked up the card, opened it, and read the simple words.

Have a great weekend,
Felix.

She froze, her stomach flipping over. Different emotions swarmed her. Surprise. Joy. Apprehension.

Gosh! What was Felix trying to do to her? Didn't she have him in her head enough already without this torture? She put the card back on the table and backed away from the bouquet. Moving over to a sofa, she sat down, still eyeing the flowers as if they were vipers.

"Ebony?" her mother probed.

"They're from Felix," she replied, her gaze still on the flowers but her mind in a thousand and one places.

"Oh, so nice," Mrs. Duru enthused. "They are absolutely beautiful, and he is such a charming young man. I think he likes you," she added with a wink.

Ebony stared at her mum, her mouth agape, heat rising to her face in embarrassment.

"Mum! Felix doesn't like me...at least, not the way you think, anyway. He is only wishing *us* a happy weekend," she said, moving her hand back and forth to emphasise the two of them, though the card hadn't said so. She didn't want her mum getting the wrong idea about her and Felix.

"I may be crippled but I'm not blind. I saw the way he looked at you when he dropped you off the other day. He likes—likes *you*, Ebony. Surely, you can see that. And with the flowers, well—"

"The flowers don't mean anything. People send other people flowers every day for all sorts of reasons. It doesn't mean it's anything romantic." The shrill words tumbled out of her lips in frustration. "I can't believe I'm having this conversation with my mother," she muttered under her breath.

Her mother laughed. "I heard that....You know, I worry about you sometimes. As a little girl, you used to dream about your wedding day. You even played bride a few times in my wedding dress. And now look at you. At the mention of a man sending you flowers, you are like a cat on a hot tin roof. What happened to my little girl?"

Her mother's face screwed up with worry lines and her eyes appealed to Ebony to tell her ate at her.

"I grew up."

And my heart got broken, crushing all my romantic dreams of a white wedding and happy ever after.

Her mum looked at her, sadness darkening her brown eyes. "My dear, I hate to see you still upset by the episode with Dele. You have to put him behind you. You have your whole life ahead of you. You should live it fully and not let people like Dele stop you from doing so."

Ebony hadn't thought she could get over the heartache of the break up with Dele. He'd been part of her whole adult life. The first and only boyfriend she'd ever had. So finding out at the last minute that he cancelled their engagement had been devastating.

After a long struggle, Dele had given in to his parents' wish that he marry someone from his ethnic group, someone they selected for him. She hadn't believed that after his promises to her of the contrary, he'd eventually caved in all because his father threatened to cut him off from his inheritance.

So much for true love. She'd learned a hard lesson but she'd learnt it well. Love only mattered when it proved convenient. She wouldn't fool herself by falling in love ever again. Didn't need the aggro. Or the heartache.

"I plan to live my life to the fullest. Dele and his ilk can't stop me. I just don't want to have any men in my life again. I can live happily without them," she emphasised as gently as she could.

Seeing the tears in her mother's eyes though, her stomach sank.

"My daughter, it is so depressing to hear you say that. Do you wish to keep punishing me? Isn't it bad enough that we lost your father and your brother—my husband and my only son? Now you tell me I'm never going to have the joy of being the mother of the bride? I'm never going to see my grandchildren before I die? It's times like this I wished your father were here."

Her mother started sniffing, tears rolling down her cheeks. Guilt flooded Ebony's mind. She quickly moved closer to her mum, kneeling in front of her and passing her the box of tissues from the coffee table.

"I'm sorry, Mum. I didn't mean to upset you." She held the older woman's hand, squeezing it tight.

Ebony could believe her own selfishness. Seeing her mum this distraught took her back to the days after the car crash that took the lives of her brother and father. Grief had bonded mother and daughter, helping them to get over their loss. Her mother's consolation had been that she had a daughter alive and well. Now that same daughter caused her grief by banishing men from her life.

"I want you to be happy." Her mother sniffed as she mopped her face with the tissue.

"And I want to make you happy, Mum." Her mind whirled. There remained only one thing that would make her mother happy right now. And she needed to stop being self-centred, for once. Her previous selfish act had resulted in the deaths in her family.

"How?" Her mum peered at her through a hand full of soggy tissues.

Ebony came to spontaneous decision.

"I have some news that will please you."

Her mum now looked at her expectantly, eyes sparkling. No turning back now.

"Felix asked me to marry him."

What have I done?

Telling her mother about Felix's proposal had seemed the best way to stop her tears at the time. Thinking on your feet, it's called.

Well, at the time, she'd been on her knees. Now, there would be no going back.

Felix would be here in any minute.

Conflicted, Ebony had dragged her feet upstairs to call him after speaking to her mother. She'd gnawed her lips with nervous energy while staring out of her bedroom windows, overlooking the back garden with its hedges of double blushing lilac hibiscus and rows of vibrant red dahlias as they'd arranged a dinner date for the same evening.

Now, as she gazed at the tight lines on her pensive reflection in the mirror on her dressing table, Ebony questioned the wisdom of her action.

"This is such a bad idea," she said out loud. "I should call him and cancel."

The image of her mother sitting on the sofa, disintegrating into tears, played back in her mind.

Groaning, she tipped her head forward into her hands bent at the elbows on the dresser and sucked in two ragged breaths.

"Mum deserves some happiness."

After the scandal and disappointment from Ebony's last unfruitful engagement, to have an actual wedding take place would be an awesome outcome.

Another long intake of breath and she lifted her head, her mind made up. Over at the closet, she withdrew two dresses.

Holding the ruffled, red, sleeveless dress against her body, she stared into the mirror.

No. A little over the top for this occasion. I don't want Felix thinking I'm coming on to him.

She flipped the dresses over, holding the black, square-neck cocktail dress up this time.

Tilting her head to one side, she frowned.

Not this one. Too conservative. I don't want him changing his mind, either.

A smile tugged at the corner of her mouth.

The sound of a car pulling into the gravel driveway caught her attention. *Felix is here already?* She glanced at her watch. *Yep, he's early!*

Stomach churning with excitement, she settled for the halter-neck, coral print dress with a waterfall hem. Feminine but understated. She slipped it on as her phone beeped with a text message.

I'm downstairs.

Felix.

Grinning and almost bouncing on her toes, she sent him a quick reply.

I'll be down soon.

Not wanting to appear too keen, she would take her time.

Staring at her well-dressed appearance in the full-length mirror sobered her up.

What am I about to do?

Fretful, she combed her fingers through her thick tresses as nervous heat enveloped her body.

Of all the impulsive things I've done in my life, this is the craziest. And I've done some rash stuff in my time.

Mangled bodies covered in dried blood floated into her mind's eye.

Panic rose, clenching her throat tight, cutting off her breathing. She slumped against the glass and fought the terror, gasping for breath. With luck, she didn't pass out as it happened sometimes when she had a panic attack.

After she regained her composure, she slipped her feet into high-heeled, snakeskin sandals, picked up her purse, and left the room.

I'm going to tell Mum the truth and call the whole thing off.

Downstairs, she walked into the formal sitting room, ready to spill the beans, and froze.

The scene displayed in front of her made her think again. Felix sat next her mother on the sofa, his back towards her. They both laughed heartily, heads tilted towards each other almost like they conspired about something. Hearing the joy in her mother's voice lifted Ebony's spirit and lips into a smile.

The first time she'd seen her laughing in a very long time. Maybe since the accident. Depression wasn't something they discussed in the open. But they'd both lived with it in varying degrees since Chidi and Dad died. She knew because her counsellor had told her years ago in her sessions.

How can I tell her the truth? It would break her heart and wipe the joy off her face. I can't do it to her.

"Oh, there you are," her mother said cheerily when she turned and noticed Ebony. "You look lovely."

"Thank you, Mum." Ebony walked over and kissed her on the cheek.

Straightening, she stepped back and her breath caught in her throat.

Felix stood tall and *ah-ma-zing* in a white linen shirt, a brilliant contrast with his dark skin, while black linen trousers clung on taut thigh muscles. The sexy dip in his cheek and gleaming eyes sent heat rushing all over her.

In two casual strides, his warm hands settled on her bare shoulders. Masculine spice cocooned her as she took a deep breath. Soft lips brushed her right cheek. Tingles skittered from the contact point, spreading south.

"Beautiful," he whispered into her ear in a low husky voice that sent lava pooling low in her body again.

She clenched her hands on her sides to stop herself from leaning into him and touching him.

Stepping back, he turned to her mum. "We have to go now, Mum. I have enjoyed our chat."

"So did I, my dear. We'll have to do it again soon. Enjoy yourselves." Her mother beamed a happy smile at them.

Ebony didn't know why but seeing the easy rapport between Felix and her mother annoyed her. Not that she didn't want him to get on with her mum. Of course, she did. It was just that she didn't want her only surviving close relative to get too close to a man who would only be a temporary fixture in their lives. If they got married and split up, it would break her mother's heart.

Felix put his arm on the curve of her back. She stiffened her spine as they walked outside in silence. His touch felt possessive, branding her skin. Would she ever get used to it?

The sun had already started on its descent into the horizon, leaving the evening sky with an eerie, orange hue. When he opened the door to his low, sleek sports car and waited for her to sit down, she couldn't help thinking about his chivalry. A smile tugged at her cheek but she determinedly banked it down. Allowing herself to get sucked into Felix's overpowering charm would be definitely a bad idea.

"What was all that about back there?" Ebony asked tartly as soon as he got into the car. She needed to keep a handle on things before they ran away from her.

"What?" Felix replied, his lips lifted at the corners with indulgent amusement. He kept his hands in a loose grip on the steering wheel as he stared out of the windshield.

Ebony crossed her arms over her chest, not amused.

Doing this whole thing is difficult enough without him joking about it. We staked my mother's happiness on this little charade, not to mention mine.

"You know what I mean...the kiss...the whole joking with my mum thing? You do realise she's going to be deeply hurt when you are no longer around." She took her seatbelt off so she could turn to face him fully, her chin raised and lips pursed in defiance.

Felix turned to her, this time his expression unreadable. He just watched her, silent, for a long moment. It seemed his eyes stripped away her veneer, looking into her soul.

"Who says I'm going anywhere?" he said at last, in a casual tone.

Their gazes locked, intense. Midnight black eyes held hers, reading her confusion. Electricity sparked between them, heating up the atmosphere. Warmth spread through her body

Snap out of it.

She shook her head and looked away, breaking the spell.

"Felix, this is hard enough as it is." He couldn't mean what she thought he meant.

He shrugged and looked out of the windscreen again. "Your mother told me about her friendship with my mother. They'd been very close." His voice sounded pensive.

"Oh, I—I d...didn't realise," she stuttered, flushed with sudden guilt.

Clenching her fist to stop from smacking her head for being selfish, she stared out of the window instead.

Mum is probably his only link to his mother outside of his family. If the two of them interacting would help Felix make peace with his mother's death, then she couldn't stop it. She had to encourage it.

We all need to make peace with our pasts. Our demons.

113

I care about him that much. Though, I don't want to care. Not again.

There. I admit it.

"About the kiss.... We are supposed to be engaged, right? I was just keeping up appearances," he said dismissively as he reached for the ignition.

"We are engaged? I haven't agreed to anything yet, you...you arrogant man." She gasped, furious at him.

"Isn't that what all this is about? Why you called me to meet up? You told your mum we were engaged, right?" His calm voice didn't hide the ticking muscle on his temple.

"H...how did you know?" Baffled, her mouth hung agape. She hadn't said anything to him on the phone except that she wanted to meet up. Did her mother ask him? Her mother wouldn't have said anything to him.

He raised his brow. "Do you have to ask?"

His hard gaze locked onto her bold one. She refused to back down, though she could have sworn he could see straight through her. His eyes softened, acquiring a glint of humour. He relented.

"The moment you called me, I knew something had happened. I'd decided not to call you but to allow you to come to your own decision. You wouldn't have called me except to agree to the deal, right?"

Dread tightened her chest, making it hard to breath.

This man could read her like a takeaway menu, easy to assimilate and discard. And he saw this only as a deal—a business transaction. It would come to an end one day. The heavy thought weighed on her mind, depressing her.

"Right," she replied with as much coolness as she could muster, though disappointed. She put her seat belt back on, leaning back into the soft, plush, cream leather bucket seat. Felix gave her one quick, curious glance before driving the car through the opened gates.

They sat upstairs in Reams Restaurant at a private corner right next to the glass, floor-to-ceiling windows

114

overlooking the hanging gardens below that were lit by spotlights. The ambiance proved relaxing, the decor elegant, with a soft jazzy music number playing through the speakers.

Apart from the waiter, there was no one else up here, though the downstairs restaurant heaved with diners. Ebony assumed Felix had arranged it so they could have some privacy. She would be horrified if anyone else overhead their discussion. He had his own worries, too. Considering his recent history with the press, preventing their conversation from being overheard and getting into the papers would be high on his list.

The waiter brought their meal and poured the champagne into their glasses, putting the bottle back in the ice bucket before leaving. They ate their meal in silence, only talking about the delicious food. She waited for Felix to bring up the topic of their fake marriage. He didn't. He studied her underneath his long, dark lashes, instead.

Steeling her body, she decided to broach the subject. She needed to talk about it before she lost her nerve. She'd spent the drive to the restaurant psyching up her mind.

"I will marry you but I have some conditions," she started, and paused for his reaction.

"What are they?"

His expression didn't change. She learned that Felix took things in easy strides. She had yet to see him riled.

"One, we remain married for two years. I can arrange to have my leave of absence extended, but two years is the maximum allowed."

He nodded in response but maintained close eye contact.

"Two, we have separate rooms during that time."

If they were going to part afterward, then there would be no point in an emotional and physical relationship, if such a thing was possible. She needed to safeguard her heart from being broken again.

At her words, something flickered in his rugged face, amusement dancing in his eyes.

"Married people make love. Why should we be any different?"

Black eyes scanned her body, trailing heat through her veins in its wake. Holding her breath, she averted her gaze so he couldn't see how he affected her.

"It will be a sham marriage. Anyway, no one will know what happens behind closed doors."

At that, he laughed, for the first time that evening; the same deep and rich laughter that always rumbled through her. Tonight, though, it didn't uplift her spirit as usual. Frustration coursed in her veins at his apparent ease with the subject of making love.

"*Ima-mmi*, remember, newlyweds are supposed to be in love. What do you think the domestic staff or worse still, the media, will make of it when they find out I haven't touched you? Because find out they surely will.... A woman who is being loved glows with that love. Haven't you ever heard that saying?"

Annoyed, she had to agree with him. Their body language would give them away. Moreover, what would the domestic staff think when they noticed she slept in separate rooms from her husband?

Tell me why this is a good idea?

"Ok, maybe not separate rooms, but separate beds in one room."

"No, that won't work, either.... What are you so afraid of? Is the idea of sharing my bed so abhorrent?"

Abhorrent? No. The image of the two of them tangled in bed sheets flashed in her head. As always, desire made her breath quicken as she pictured Felix touching her, kissing her. Her body had no problems with sharing a bed with him. It welcomed the pleasurable idea.

The thought racked her mind with dismay, while her heart feared the implications.

I've only every made love to one man in my life and I loved him with my whole being. If she surrendered her body to Felix, her heart would follow suit. Where would this leave her in two years when he walked away?

116

He'll take a piece of me with him. I can't let that happen.

"If it's your wish that we don't have any intimacy through our marriage, then I won't force the issue. Nevertheless, remember this. I find you very desirable. If you change your mind, you know where I'll be."

His lips lifted in a teasing smile. He held her hand, using his thumb to slowly caress her knuckles.

Felix desired her? That knowledge spread more warmth through her body, converging low in her belly. The thing he did on her hand wasn't helping, either. He left the choice of whether they slept together to her but truthfully, she'd have to call on her reserves of strength if she were to withstand him whilst sleeping in the same bed. She pulled her hand and he let it go. Ebony leaned back into her chair, putting some distance between them.

"Where will that be?" she asked curiously.

"Right next to you, in our bed, of course."

His seductive smile told her about all the possibilities entailed within that promise.

"Fine. Same room, same bed, but pillows between us, and you keep to your side." She would keep her body as far away from him as possible.

"Fine." His smile lost some of its sparkle. He waved his hand in the air, leaning back into his chair. Could he be angry she wouldn't give in to making love?

"Any other conditions?" he asked, lifted his hand in a languid wave.

"Yes. Whatever we tell my mother when we break up, I want to tell her myself. I know she will be upset, but I want to speak to her privately first to prepare her for the actual break up when the time comes.... That's it."

She bit her lower lip, self-consciously looking away from Felix as she tried to gather her thoughts. He wasn't happy to meet her conditions. Where did that leave them? They were now automatically engaged? She turned back to ask him but stopped when Felix stood. Without saying anything, he came round to her and pulled her up into his arms.

117

As she gasped with shock, her pulse raced off on an unexpected sprint. Mesmerised, she watched him lower his head, then his lips brushed hers in a slow, sensual kiss. His tongue slid around the edges of her lips before probing for entry.

Without reservation, she opened up, welcoming him. Sighing, she gave herself to the kiss, moving her hand up his chest. She stepped closer to him, her soft body flush against his hard frame. She felt his groan as he deepened the kiss, taking her tongue on an exhilarating tango. Tingles of heat skittered across her skin. Her knees buckled, and she clutched his taut, muscular arms for balance.

Felix lifted his head, his ragged breath fanning her face. She noted the pulse at the base of his neck beating frantically. She certainly wasn't the only one affected by the overwhelming kiss.

"I did promise."

The huskiness of his voice sent shivers down her spine. Desire-filled midnight eyes watched her lips with hunger. His hand, still tangled in her hair, caressed her nape gently.

Her forehead furrowed in confusion. Her brain must be frazzled from the kiss because she didn't understand his words. "You promised?"

With his other hand, he ran his index finger across her lower lip like he was soothing it. "To kiss your lips better each time you bit them." He smiled with arrogance. "I keep my promises."

Her mind became awash with the naughty possibilities. She hadn't realised he meant it. That he would carry out his sweet threat—his promise.

"You do realise I bite my lips a lot, especially when I'm nervous or thinking," she said, out of breath.

"In which case, I'll be spending a lot of time kissing your sweet lips better."

Pure masculine enjoyment played on sensuous lips. Deep longing unfurled within her.

"We'll never get anything done." Her smile widened at the thought of Felix interrupting his planned activities just to kiss her each time she bit her lips.

"On the contrary, I can think of wonderful and pleasurable things we could accomplish together." He leaned back to sweep his gaze over her body, leaving a trail of heat behind. "The lips are only the start. The rest of you will need attention, too."

Her mouth formed an O in astonishment. Surely, he wasn't serious. As if reading her mind, he winked naughtily and sat her back on the chair before taking his seat.

"So here's to us." He lifted his glass of champagne. "And a happy married life."

"To us," Ebony said soberly, hoping she wasn't making the worst mistake of her life—that her marriage to Felix would be happy.

CHAPTER EIGHT

"So you see? This is all staged," Ebony told Faith as tears pooled in her eyes, blurring her vision.

Her friend came over and hugged her.

"Are you not mad at me for keeping the secret from you?" She eyed her friend.

"Of course, I'm disappointed you didn't tell me this earlier." Faith leaned back to stared at her face. "But I understand the need for secrecy with something like this. If it gets out, it'll be bad all round. And moreover, we've all got secrets. So I can't hold it against you."

Momentary relief flooded Ebony. She couldn't afford to lose her best friend when she needed her most.

"I wish Felix would be as forgiving when he finds out the truth." She reached for her glass of water.

"Your relationship may have started out as business arrangement. But it can change," her friend said in a matter-of-fact tone.

"Felix would be so angry if the test is positive. He was quite adamant about having no children as a clause in the pre-nuptial agreement." She stared at the hallway door, her hands shaking from nervousness.

"Listen, you need to stop stressing. First things first, we need to see the result of the test. It could be negative."

"And—"

Faith cut her off. "And if it's not, we'll sit down, think about things clearly, and deal with it. There is always a way. So shall we go and check it?"

"I don't even think I can bear to look. Can you check it for me, please?" Ebony swiped the tears with the back of her hand.

"Okay. We'll go to the bathroom together and I'll check the kit for you. How's that?"

Ebony nodded, dread weighing heavy on her shoulders. When they got to the bathroom, Faith picked up the stick. She held out her other hand and squeezed Ebony's fingers reassuringly.

"Okay. Don't panic, but it is positive." Faith squeezed her hand again. "We can do another test, just to be sure."

Feeling faint, Ebony shook her head. "No. It will still come up positive. I am pregnant."

The words felt strange on her tongue, her mind woozy. She sat on the covered toilet seat and lowered her head. She let the confirmation wash over her. Being pregnant wasn't bad news to her. It would be bad news for her relationship with Felix, a relationship she wanted to keep.

"What am I going to do?" She voiced her despondent thoughts.

Faith massaged her back with gentle care. "Let's go sit in the sofa and we can decide what to do next."

Her calm voice cut through Ebony's panicked mind.

In the living room, Faith brought her a glass of water. Ebony took a sip, the cool liquid soothing her dry throat.

"What are things like with Felix at the moment?" Faith enquired in a matter-of-fact manner.

Ebony focused her thoughts, remembering the events of the last few months with Felix. "Things have been absolutely wonderful. Before we got married, he'd been so cold and withdrawn. I'd thought he wouldn't show up on our wedding day."

Ebony's eyes clouded over with pain as she recalled those horrible days when she'd been so worried Felix would cancel the wedding at the last minute. She'd dreaded it would be like Dele all over again. She'd been so relieved when the wedding had gone ahead. But then, disaster had struck on their wedding night.

"Since he woke up, he is almost like a different man. Of course, the fact he can't remember meeting or marrying me could be the reason."

"What? He can't remember you." Faith stared at her wide-eyed.

"Sorry, that's another thing I had to keep quiet. Felix has amnesia."

"Seriously?" Her friend covered her mouth.

Ebony nodded. "The day he woke up from the coma, he didn't recognise me. It was a nightmare."

"I can imagine."

"And also a blessing in disguise. He has been kind, gentle, and loving. I swear to you, Faith. Like he loves me. You should see the way he behaved last night. He practically worshipped my body."

"Girl, I think you are confusing great sex with love."

Ebony understood her friend's scepticism. Faith had a difficult life growing up; it had made her close off her heart to sentiments.

It didn't stop Ebony from glaring at her friend with defiance. "I think I can tell the difference, thank you. What we did last night and this morning, we made sweet love. My body is still humming just thinking about it." Ebony hugged her body again, a smile tugging at her lips. "Seriously, though, he's been amazing, generally. But then, I keep thinking he's going to remember everything and things are going to go back to how it was. With this pregnancy, it's going to be even worse now."

"If he has been as great as you say he has, then, it might not be as bad as you think if you tell him. He might actually welcome it as a way of sealing you newfound love." Faith waved her hand in the air to emphasise her point.

Our newfound love that's about to die an untimely death in its infancy.

"I hope he sees it that way. I don't want to lose Felix but I want this baby, too. Is that too much to ask?"

"No, it's not. Talk to him. I'm sure he'll understand. It's not as if you planned it. Just make sure you tell him first before he finds out himself. Okay?"

Ebony nodded, glancing at her watch. "Oh, gosh. Is that the time? I have to go. I only said I'd pop out to the shops quickly. We are supposed to be going to the beach for the day. He'll wonder where I've gone."

She stood up and picked up her handbag.

"Well, have fun and call me if you need reinforcements." Her friend smiled at her reassuringly.

Ebony gave her a quick hug and raced downstairs to her car.

Outside in the garden, Felix sat on the bench under the shade of the acacia tree, his favourite spot in his vast estate. Eyes closed; still he became aware of Ebony before she reached him or spoke. The swish of her dress as she moved, and the patter of her footsteps against the cobbles of the stone path that weaved through the back garden announced her presence. As she approached, he smelled her essence. He didn't open his eyes. Instead, he inhaled deeply as his body stirred.

"Hi, darling." Soft lips brushed his in a brief kiss.

Within his body, desire sparked. Alarm bells rang in his mind. His spine stiffened with suspicion. She called him "darling." She'd never used that word on him before. Something must be definitely wrong.

Eyes opened, he stared at her through his dark sunglasses. A smile curled her beautiful lips, but her usual radiant glow seemed diminished, somehow. Dark sunshades covered her eyes so he couldn't see them. Loose, dark curls lay swept over one shoulder, her dress a sea-blue sundress that showed off long, smooth legs.

His body didn't care what she'd been up to. He wanted to sit her on his lap right here and sink into her wet core. To rock into her and make her forget whatever could be on her mind. He wanted her to bare all to him. To hide nothing from his gaze, from him. To hear her cry out his name over and over again like she'd done this morning.

Drawing in a long breath, he controlled his baser urges. He wouldn't be reduced to an animal regardless of how much she pushed him. Actions borne out of rage had resulted in his accident. Evidence that he'd already lost himself to his wife if whatever they'd argued about had resulted in him storming out.

Moreover, he had other things to consider. Even as his house sat enclosed and not overlooked, his security team were out there. Not visible, but still out there. Watching in silence.

"Did you get everything you needed?" he asked instead. He wondered how much she would tell him.

"Yes. And I stopped over to see Faith quickly." She sat down next to him, her warmth enfolding his body.

"Faith?" he asked, his nonchalant manner belying his raging emotions.

"Yes. You remember Faith? My best friend? I was telling you about her this morning. You met her at Reams. She was my maid of honour on our wedding day. You've seen her picture on the wedding album."

The knot in his stomach tightened. A rambling Ebony only heightened his suspicion. Maintaining his outward calm, he nodded.

"Okay. Now I remember. How is she?" He watched her lips, fighting the urge to pull her closer and savour their sweetness. The same lips hiding truths from him. He swallowed the bile in his throat and looked away from her.

"She is fine. Are you ready to go?" Her voice remained cool but he didn't miss the way her hand on the bench tightened with tension.

"Sure. You get organised. I'll meet you inside. Pack a bag, too. I've decided we should stay overnight at the resort." He hoped the time away with just the two of them would help her open up to him. One way or the other, he would find out what she hid. He hated secrets.

"Great. Don't be long." She stood and strolled off back into the house.

He took out his phone from his pocket and typed a message.

What's the report?

The response back read: *She drove to the local pharmacist, to her friend's house in Lekki, and then she came straight back home.*

Felix let out a breath he hadn't realised he'd been holding, relief flushing his mind. Ebony had told him the truth about her whereabouts. Yet, some of the tension remained in his body. He still couldn't shake the feeling something was wrong.

He stood up and walked into the house.

Ebony pushed her current dilemma to the back of her mind. Not much she could do about it at the moment. Instead, she focused on sorting out the picnic items and things they needed for their day away.

Fragile and uncertain about her future with Felix, she debated about telling him she was pregnant that night but settled on revealing it to him the next morning. Wanting to spend one more day with the loving Felix eclipsed her sense of guilt and responsibility. After months of stumbling from one disaster to another, she needed a break from the hell to be unleashed when she spilled the beans.

On the drive out to *La Campagne Tropicana*, a remote beach resort on the outskirts of Lagos State, Kola drove the car, which surprised her, considering Patrick was the usual driver. When Felix spoke, she suddenly understood the need for the change.

"When I was a boy, my father cheated on my mother."

She gasped, turning in her seat to look at him. Felix wasn't looking at her, his gaze focused on a point on the blacked out windows of the Porsche Cayenne whizzing down the expressway.

Why would he reveal something like this out of the blue?

"It wasn't just a one-off affair," he continued. "He would spend days away and when I asked my mother, she would say he travelled on business. He kept it a secret for a long time."

The pain wrapped up in his words knifed through her. She reached for him, covering his hand with hers. "I'm so sorry."

He turned around staring at her hand as if not really seeing it.

"Have you ever wondered why there's only a two year gap between Mark and I? After all, my mum died when I was eight."

She frowned. "I've never really thought about it. I always assumed your dad married Mark's mother after your mum passed on."

"You are correct. They did get married afterwards. But while my mother was alive, they were having an affair. Mark is the product of that affair."

"Oh." She didn't know what else to say.

Beneath her fingers, his hand clenched tight into a fist but he didn't withdraw it and she was grateful he chose to maintain contact.

"You see, it broke my mother's heart finding out what my father did. I would watch her crying day after day. As a boy, I swore I would never get married. Never put myself through such vulnerability and heart ache."

Shadows clouded his eyes and his chest rose as he drew a long breath.

"Then I met you and broke that vow because I care about you. I feel as if I've known you all my life when as you say it has only been months. I know we are meant to be together."

She lowered her gaze. He reached across and tipped her head back up with his finger under her chin.

"I know it as much as I know the sun will set tonight. But you've got to trust me and share the things bothering this pretty head of yours." He brushed back strands of hair from her face.

She relaxed into him, some of her earlier anxiety fleeing her body. The physical contact with Felix always seemed to soothe her nerves.

"Felix, I—"

He ran his tongue around the edges of her lips, inflaming her. When his tongue probed her mouth for entry, she sighed and opened up her lips, letting him in. He thrust into her with determination and promise, and her uncertainty dissolved in a haze of passion. She remained eager for his touch to soothe her jangled nerves, suddenly needing to be closer to Felix. To hear him say her name with fervour. To feel wanted and loved. He wanted her. That proved certain. Did her love her? This morning, she would have said yes, but now, she didn't feel so confident. Not with an unexpected pregnancy looming over them.

Her excitement rose as he moved his lips to her chin, neck, and eventually, her ear, sensitising her body.

The car slowed as they arrived at their destination, stopping their play. Felix had booked a villa for the day. It turned out to be a large, luxury hut built from wood and filled with indulgent mod-cons, located in a secluded corner of the resort and surrounded by long, shaded palm trees, the white sandy beach, and the deep blue ocean only a few metres away. The clear water of the private swimming pool sparkled next to the hut.

After the resort staff left, Ebony went into the bathroom and changed into her red bikini, tying a gauzy black sarong around her waist. She pulled her hair back, holding it in place with a band. When she came out from the bathroom, Felix had already changed into a pair of navy blue swimming shorts and a loose, sky blue shirt with the buttons undone. He sat outside on the wooden beach lounger, his leg cast covered in a waterproof protector.

"I've dismissed everyone so we've got the whole place to ourselves. What would you like to do first?"

"As much as that sea beckons, I'll settle for the swimming pool for now." Ebony left her towel on the deck chair and took off her sarong. "Are you coming?" She flashed him a teasing look and dived into the water, swimming to the other end.

When she turned around, Felix was beside her in the pool. She swam past him towards the other end.

"Oh, yeah? Are we racing?" he asked, his brow raised in amusement.

She just laughed and kept going. His injured leg didn't seem to be giving him much difficulty under the water as he kept close to her. They swam a few more laps before he grabbed her arm.

"I'm tired of playing chase. I'm hungry." The husky edge in his deep voice raised the hair on her neck and arms. Nipples beaded and heart thumping, she turned to face him. The fire in his eyes heated her body up.

"Okay. I'll dry up and sort out lunch," she replied, licking her lips.

He chuckled and tugged until they were only separated by wet swimsuits. The hard evidence of his arousal pulsated against her tummy.

"Not that kind of food," his voice rumbled in a growl. "I mean to have you for lunch."

Felix crushed his lips against Ebony's. He heard her breath hitch. He didn't ease up. The kiss turned punishing, vengeful. All his frustration at her for hiding things from him registered in that gesture. She returned the kiss but it wasn't a surrender; more like a duelling of tongues, a battle of wills. As he cut and thrust, she defended and parried, matching his every move.

His already inflamed blood fizzed in his veins. The intensity of his need consumed him. His hand moved down to her inner thighs, shoving the bikini aside. His finger thrust into her wet folds, checking for her readiness. She lay wet and slick, her juices coating his finger. He added another, and another. He knew he should be gentler, slower, but the thing thrumming in his blood wasn't love and tenderness, but anger and envy.

Ebony didn't seem to care because she thrust her hips towards him and moved her hand into his shorts, massaging his arousal. At that point, the thin control he tried reining in shredded into nothing. He needed her now. Needed to cool his fizzing blood before he went mad. He'd wanted her all afternoon, and seeing her walk out of that bathroom in nothing but a skimpy red bikini had been like a red flag to a bull. She had teased him even more by starting the race in the pool. Enough was enough.

He moved her to the edge of the pool for anchor. She moaned and wrapped her long legs around his waist. He ripped her bikini off, lifted her up, and sank into her moist depths. A deep groan erupted from his belly.

With his hands on her hips, he pulled out of her and thrust in. Again and again and again. She held onto his shoulders and met each thrust, her head thrown back in abandon. He took one breast in his mouth and suckled. She moaned with pleasure. Their breathing got shorter and harder. He could feel her excitement building to match his. He wanted to hear his name on her lips in ecstasy. Bracing one hand behind her on the edge of the pool, he moved the other to her swollen nub and pressed the tip. He felt her splinter. Her insides contracted, pulling him in, his name on her lips rapturous. With one final thrust, he spilled his seed inside her.

When he finally got his breath back, Ebony was hanging onto him, her head on his shoulder. He lifted her out of the water, sitting her on the edge of the pool. After hoisting himself out, he pulled a towel off the chair and wrapped it around her before tying one around his waist.

He sat on the deck chair and lifted her onto his lap. She leaned onto his chest. They both lay there silently and he caressed her body slowly until he heard her fall into a light sleep.

As he drifted into sleep, his brain opened up that place his conscious mind had placed under lock and key. Bright light slowly filtered into a dark room, revealing a young boy in a park chanting the words over and over again. *Felix loves Ebony.*

CHAPTER NINE

The sound of something vibrating on a hard surface woke Felix. He opened his eyes. His phone sat on the wooden table next to him, just out of reach. Ebony still slept on him, her arms wrapped around him. She looked so peaceful he didn't want to wake her by moving. The vibrations continued. He wanted to ignore the phone but it could be something important. He'd been expecting a call back from Mark.

When he sat up, Ebony stirred, opening her golden eyes, and smiled at him sleepily. She looked so beautiful his heart rammed in his chest. He held her head and kissed her deeply. Warm blood thrummed in his veins. When he pulled back, her eyes had darkened with yearning. Knowing how responsive she could be to him, he smiled with satisfaction.

"Is that your phone?" She turned in the direction of the buzzing device, her lips lifted in a smile.

"Yep. Whoever is on the other end is pretty insistent. I better get it." He rubbed his knuckles against her cheeks.

She stood up. "And I'll get dressed and sort out lunch. I'm so hungry I could eat a horse."

His eyebrows quirked up and he chuckled. "A horse?"

"Figuratively, of course." She laughed before sashaying inside, the short towel around her displaying long, smooth legs that had been wound around him not too long ago. His body tightened in response.

The buzzing phone stopped him from following her indoors. He picked it up and saw the name on the caller display. Mark.

"At last," Mark said when he answered. "I've been trying to reach you. Got your message."

"I just wondered if you were free to meet up. I've got a few things I want to run by you," Felix replied, turning his back to the door Ebony had disappeared into as he tried to dispel her image from his mind.

"I'm currently in Jo'burg and won't be back in Lagos for a couple of days. But I can talk now."

"This is not a conversation for the phone. Will you be back by Friday?" Felix couldn't afford anyone else overhearing his telephone conversation. The last thing he needed right now was another media scandal. Moreover, he wanted to talk to Ebony first. Give her the opportunity to come clean about what sat on her mind.

"Yes. We could meet at the usual place," Mark replied.

"Good. Same time, too. See you then."

"Ok. Bye."

Felix switched his phone off and went inside to find his wife.

Whilst Felix was outside, Ebony showered quickly and got dressed in a white top and red Capri trousers. As she stood in front of the mirror, she placed a hand on her still flat tummy, a loving smile on her face. A little life grew inside her. A life that was nothing more than a mass of cells at the moment. But to her, a life, nonetheless.

Too many people had gone from her life. Too many lives lost because of circumstances beyond her control. Her father. Her brother. Taken because she had chosen a love affair with the wrong person over her family. A love affair with Dele Savage. In the end, she'd lost the people that mattered to her and still lost Dele.

Now, it seemed she faced another unpalatable dilemma. She had the tiny life within her that she wanted desperately. Yet, she also had to consider Felix, whom she would give anything to have forever. Well, almost anything. Felix was only supposed to be her husband for two years. That had been the deal. This new life growing within her represented new beginnings for her. For Felix, too, if he'd give them a chance.

She wanted to keep both of them. But how possible would that be? She would have to try and convince him that they were worth it. That their relationship could foster the right environment for a child to grow and flourish. That what they had amounted to more than just a business deal that would end one day. However, before she told him, she'd have to show him first. So that when she said the words, he'd believe her. Hopefully.

Ebony walked into the kitchen and picked up the lunch items she'd brought along. More scenic and romantic eating outside, so she arranged the items on the table set under the shade of the palm trees. From here, they'd have an unobstructed view of the sea.

Felix came out holding the bottle of chilled white wine and the wine glasses. He'd dressed in grey combat shorts and a white t-shirt that clung to his muscular torso. Ebony had to stop herself from reaching out to touch his chest.

"I thought we'd eat out here. It's shaded and cool. Plus I love watching and listening to the crash of the sea waves on the sand," she said, averting her eyes from the object of her distraction.

"Sure. That's the whole point of being out here. Get away from the distractions of Lagos and enjoy the solace and tranquillity of the beach." He moved his chair closer to her and sat down before pouring the wine.

"It's just lovely being out here. The sound of the sea is so soothing, the cool breeze refreshing, and the fact we can have this section of the beach all to ourselves is great, too. I'm surprised we haven't had any intruders."

She started dishing out the food. He took one of her hands and placed a kiss on the centre of her palm. A bolt of electricity shot through her.

"For the right price, we could have the whole stretch of beach," he said as he shrugged with nonchalance before fixing her with a concerned stare. "I was hoping the break away from your normal routine would get you to relax and stop worrying. I know the past few weeks must have been difficult for you, but things are going to get better. If only you'd trust me."

His unreadable dark eyes held hers in a trance. For a moment, she remained tongue-tied as her pulse picked up. If only she could trust him completely, but this would be just a bubble. When his memory came back, this illusion would end. She had to protect herself from the fallout sure to happen.

"Felix, I...I trust you," she lied.

"Do you?" he asked ruefully as he caressed her cheek. His eyes told her he saw through her lie. "Maybe not today, but hopefully, one day soon. For now, I want to thank you for all your prayers and for staying with me when others would have given up hope." He kissed her palm again, sending more tingles down her arm.

"You don't need to thank me. Where else would I have been but besides you? I am your wife."

"That you are. And a good wife, too, from all accounts." His smile radiated charm, melting her insides.

"Accounts? Who's been talking to you about me?" She laughed nervously, her sense of guilt making her body tremble.

A shadow of sadness flickered in his eyes. "You have been, though, haven't you? A good wife?"

Knots twisted in Ebony's belly, her heart skipping a beat. She lowered her eyes to the plates of food and forked a piece of chicken in her salad. Did Felix sense something amiss? She had withheld things from him. About their marriage. About the life growing in her. Did that make her a bad wife?

"You tell me. It's for you to decide. Am I a good wife?" She kept her eyes averted, not wanting him to see her guilt.

His warm laughter floated in the sea breeze.

"I like that. Throw that back at me, won't you? From the smell of the food, I'd say you are a very good wife. How's that?" He winked at her. The humour in his voice settled some of her worry.

"Is that all it takes to please you? Cook you a nice meal?" she smiled tentatively.

"That's a good start. Although I can think of plenty more ways you please me, too."

His gaze scanned her body in that way that spelled pure Felix and so masculine. Her skin flushed with heat as she remembered the two of them in the pool. What if someone had seen them? She had been so overcome by the moment that she hadn't noticed anything else. Just Felix. His potent masculinity and her primal need to connect with him, to soothe her jangled nerves with his roaring possession.

She'd noticed his cool aloofness back in the house when she'd returned from Faith's house. That remoteness had remained all day except for the brief spell in the car when he'd kissed her before they arrived at the resort. She'd felt she needed to do something to draw him out. Wearing that bikini had been calculated but it worked. He took the bait and the result had been the fiercest trip to ecstasy she'd ever taken. A shiver of excitement slid down her spine.

"I hope I'll continue to please you." *Even after you find out the truth about us.* She looked up and smiled at him boldly.

He smiled at her. "Of course you will."

He speared some of the food and fed her. They ate and talked jovially. About nothing serious; the food, the resort, the beach, sports. They quibbled cheerily about which proved the better sports—American football versus rugby—Ebony supporting the former and Felix the latter.

After lunch, they strolled along the beach arm-in-arm. Felix held her close. When they got to a shaded cove, they both got down on the sand. She sat in front of Felix, between his thighs, and leaned back against his chest, basking in his warmth, his firmness, his strength. It felt so good being with him. She wanted the feeling to last forever. They sat there watching the fishermen in their boats on the horizon.

"Tell me about you. What were you like as a child?" Felix asked her as he stroked her arms with tenderness.

"If you want to find out what I was like as a child, you might want to talk to Mum. She'll bring out all the old photos and bore you to death." She laughed and Felix joined her.

"My brother and I were both born in Lagos, although we travelled around a lot depending on where my father got posted. We eventually moved to the USA, where we settled when I was about twelve years old. My childhood was very happy, Chidi being about four years my senior. He was a good brother. Overprotective sometimes, but still good. We were a happy family. It all changed later, all because of me. Then Dad and Chidi died."

Ebony shivered as the memories descended on her. As if sensing her unease, Felix pulled her closer, wrapping his arms around her.

"You know, I think I remember Chidi. We were about the same age. I think I remember playing football with him as a kid."

Felix kept a cheery tone. A blanket of anguish enclosed Ebony, almost suffocating her. She lowered her head into her hands. Felix took her hands away and pulled her into his chest.

"I know the memories hurt," he said in a soothing voice. "If you want to stop, that's fine by me. But I think talking about it would help you to bury the past finally." He caressed her back. She sighed as some of the tension left her body.

"I know. I want to talk about it," she murmured.

"How did things change?"

He spoke quietly and affectionately, holding her tightly. She felt safe. Secure.

"Things changed when I met Dele. My first year at university, and I'd just turned eighteen. We met at a campus party. He was a medical student in his fourth year—sporty, very popular, and good-looking. I guess I fell in love with him on sight. When he asked me out on a date,

I couldn't believe my luck. I hadn't dated anybody previously, so I guess I proved naive about relationships. I was willing to do whatever it took to keep him happy. He became the centre of my focus outside of my studies. He more or less controlled everything I did. When my parents found out about our relationship, they tried to discourage me. Said I should focus on my studies and leave relationships for after graduation. As far as I was concerned, I had met the man of my dreams and we were going to live happily ever after."

The memories swam in her mind as if she lived through them again. Felix continued his gentle caress on her shoulders and arms. She exhaled another deep breath.

"When Dele decided to come to Nigeria to see his parents, he invited me to come along. I knew my parents wouldn't let me go, so I didn't tell them and came to Nigeria with Dele. Whilst there, I found out his parents didn't like me. They excluded me from conversations by only speaking Yoruba, a language they knew I couldn't understand. At the time, I put it down to their idiosyncrasy and Dele dismissed it as nothing, so I forgot about it."

Her heart contracted in pain, and tears stung the back of her eyes. She squeezed her eyes shut.

"My parents found out about my trip to Nigeria. They came there in search of me. On their way to the Savages' house, the accident happened. A huge fuel tanker with bad brakes careered into their car, killing my brother who was driving. My father died later in the hospital. Though I never got there in time to see him."

The tears ran freely down her cheeks. Felix's hold on her body tightened. He rocked her, whispering calming words in her ear.

"It's ok, *ima-mmi*. It's over now."

When her sobs quietened, she spoke again. "Dele's mother told me about the accident. They'd received a call from the hospital. My mother had their contact details. Though her injuries were crippling, she'd been awake and able to talk.... If I hadn't come to Nigeria, that accident would never have happened. It was my fault. I killed my father and brother. And crippled my mother."

"No. The accident wasn't your fault. I won't have you blame yourself," he spoke gruffly against her hair. He turned her face, his expression determined. "It wasn't your fault. Okay?"

His conviction calmed her down. Relief spread through her that he didn't judge her as guilty. She nodded and continued.

"After the accident, Dele and I got even closer. He was very good to me, supported me through the period my mother was in hospital and through the funeral. We talked about marriage several times but some obstacle always crept up. First, he wanted to finish medical school. Then, it became his residency. Then he wanted to work for a while, earn some money, and make a name for himself. I waited patiently, thinking that as long as I was with the man I loved, it would all come together. Eventually, two years ago, he bought me a ring and proposed. I was so happy. We set a date. Finally, everything came together. My mother was happy that he would finally make an honest woman out of me. However, the euphoria didn't last. A month to our wedding date, he told me he couldn't go through with it. His father had threatened to disown him if he married me. I wasn't the right person for him. They had a more suitable candidate. Basically, it boiled down to the fact that I came from a different ethnic group. I was devastated. What about all we'd been through together? All the years I'd committed to him? All the promises he made to me? Did those count for nothing? Did he not love me enough? Well, apparently not.

"So when my mother started talking about a ten-year memorial service for my dad and Chidi, as much as I didn't want to return here, I had to come back. To finally lay their ghosts to rest. To finally move on with my life. My plan spelled to forget about men and concentrate on my career. Of course, I never reckoned on you." She smiled weakly. "From the moment I saw you at the airport, you've been like a force of nature razing everything in your path. Then you asked me to marry you and had everything all planned out until your accident happened. I got so scared and thought, not again. It felt like replaying history. Another life-altering car crash. Lord knows what I would have done if you hadn't lived. Getting that phone call to say you were awake was the best news I'd ever had." She wriggled closer to him, so glad he was alive and on the mend.

"I'm not going anywhere. You have to believe that," he said huskily against her cheek.

"In my life, I have watched the people I love get injured and die because of my stupidity. When your accident happened, I blamed myself. I thought I must be cursed. That there had to be something inherently wrong with me."

Tears pooled in her eyes again and he kissed each drop tenderly as they fell on her cheeks.

"There's nothing wrong with you. You are a beautiful, intelligent, passionate, kind, and generous young woman. Waking up to find you in my life has been wonderful and I wouldn't change it. I feel I have been given a new lease on life all because of you. For the first time in a very long time, I am happy, and it's all you, *ima-mmi*."

His tender words warmed her heart, dissolving her despondency. Felix was happy being with her. She hoped things would only get better.

"Being with you these past few days has more than made up for the pain of the past. But you're welcome to show me how happy you are later."

He chuckled and pulled her in for a kiss so tender that she melted on the spot. But it was over too quickly. Felix stood and pulled her up. They headed back to the hut.

That evening, they dined under the stars to the sound of the waves crashing and the saltiness of the light sea breeze on their lips. Felix fed her the delicious, fresh seafood from the platter. The food had been prepared in front of them in an open fire. Later that night, when it became just the two of them in the hut, Felix made love to her tenderly, softly whispering words of endearment, showering her body with adoration. Replete, she slept off in his arms, feeling contented and cherished. Several times in the night, they woke and each time, the lovemaking proved passionate and fulfilling. They made love at dawn once more and when Ebony woke later, the sun was already up, and Felix not in bed.

She got out of bed. With nothing else within reach, she put on Felix's shirt in a hurry to find him. It looked big on her and came down to her mid-thighs. She walked out to the decked area to find Felix getting out of the swimming pool. The water droplets glistened off his body and he picked up a towel and wrapped it around his waist.

"How did you sleep?" he asked her and smiled warmly as he walked towards her.

"Very well, considering." She returned the smile, strolling over to him.

"You look sexy in my shirt." He kissed her hungrily before pulling back. "I've ordered breakfast. It'll be here any minute. I've got a huge appetite this morning." He kissed her again, his tongue sweeping her lips.

At that point, two stewards turned up with trays of food and drinks and laid them on the table outside. When they left, Felix took her hand and led her to the table, sitting her on his lap. He fed her like he'd done the previous morning, ensuring she ate some of the food. She ate as much as she could, not wanting to make him suspicious even though she didn't have any appetite for a hearty meal.

When they finished eating, Felix's phone started buzzing and she used the opportunity to escape to the bathroom when she felt nauseous. After throwing up, she straightened up when she felt Felix's hand on her back, massaging it lightly. Panicked for a moment, she hadn't realised that he'd heard her or come into the bathroom. She should have known the sounds would carry through the internal walls. He poured some water from the tap into a glass and gave it to her. She rinsed out her mouth, took a deep breath, and turned to face him.

"Ebony, what's wrong with you. Are you sick?" Felix's handsome face creased with worry.

She shook her head. "I'm not sick. I'm fine."

He stepped back and scrubbed his head with his hand. "You're not fine. You are thin. You don't eat. And the food you eat, you throw it back up." His eyes narrowed in suspicion. "It's not some kind of eating disorder, is it?"

She laughed nervously, looking away from him. If only. How would she tell him that this wasn't an illness or disorder? That it was just her body's way of adjusting to the new life growing inside her? A new life she knew he would surely reject.

"So if it isn't that, what is it?"

"Felix, I...."

He suddenly stood rock still, his hands frozen mid-air as he reached for her. His eyes darkened, his skin draining of blood as he seemed to make a realisation.

"Are you pregnant?"

CHAPTER TEN

Felix watched Ebony as she blanched and gripped the sink tighter. Overtaken by a mixed feeling of disgust and anguish, he felt like his heart was being ripped out of his chest when he saw her nod. He was right. She was pregnant. She looked pale. He should pull her closer just in case she fell, but he couldn't move his limbs for some reason.

"And you let me touch you," he gritted out, his fists clenched beside his body. An image of all the things he'd done to her body flashed in his mind, sickening him. He couldn't bear to look at her, so he turned and walked out of the bathroom.

"Felix, please let me explain."

He heard her stricken voice behind him but he didn't turn to look at her. Neither did he stop. Instead, he picked up his shirt and walked out of the hut.

He walked along the beach, pain twisting his stomach in knots. Ebony, pregnant. Why had she let him touch her? He'd used no protection. She being his wife, he'd assumed no reason for them to have a barrier between them. Yet, there existed another life growing inside her.

Did she still love her ex-fiancé? Did she want him back? She'd told him they hadn't had a wedding night. He'd assumed that meant they hadn't made love previously. Had yesterday been the first time they'd had sex? Surely, she would have told him if the child was his? She wouldn't have hidden this from him.

He turned and went back towards the hut. He had to find out the truth once and for all. He just didn't know what he would do if the child wasn't his. If she'd been with someone else in such a short time before their wedding.

Could this be linked to why they didn't have a wedding night?

He walked into the bedroom and saw her sitting on the bed, her head in her hands. He yearned to go to her and pick her up in his arms. But he decided against it. He needed a clear head to think without the distractions of her soft body against him. Instead, he pulled up a chair and sat astride it, facing her. He wanted to see her face when she answered his questions.

"How long have you known about the pregnancy?" The words out of his mouth were hollow and forced, but they came out, anyway.

She lifted her head up. There were no tears in her eyes. Instead, they had a fire in them, a determination he hadn't seen before.

"Yesterday morning. I'd been throwing up for a few days, but it's only yesterday that I suspected it could be something other than an upset tummy. So I bought the kit and did the test at Faith's house. It turned out positive."

It all clicked together. All her cloak and dagger movements yesterday morning. A thought occurred to him. Since she hadn't talked to him about the pregnancy, she would have told her ex. Right now, he hated the fact he couldn't remember all the events leading up to their marriage. Would he have still married Ebony if he'd know she could be carrying someone else's child?

"Do you want him back? Does he know?" It hurt to ask, but he had to know.

"Does who know?" She looked at him, her eyes widened in confusion.

"The father of the child. You ex-fiancé, I presume."

"You think I've been with someone else? What kind of person do you think I am?" Her brown eyes flashed at him furiously. "There's been no one else since you."

His disdainful laugh echoed off the wooden walls. "Unless you are about to tell me that by some miracle of nature, my sperm has been so effective that you have conceived in under twenty-four hours, I would suggest quite

144

adamantly that someone else is involved. So much for trying to give you the benefit of the doubt."

He stood up, disgust and anger bubbling in his veins, and stepped away from the chair.

"For your information, Lord High and Mighty, yesterday wasn't the first time we slept together."

Every fibre in his body froze at her contemptuous words and he glared at her.

"What are you saying?"

"We made love on the night of the Governor's ball in Calabar two weeks before we got married."

The day before the Governor's Christmas Ball.

Felix and Ebony arrived together in Calabar for the Governor's Charity Ball, an annual event the Essiens had been attending for years. Calabar was the Essiens' hometown and they enjoyed a status close to royalty as their family line could be traced back generations to the earliest settlers on the estuary. Felix also served as the patron to several local charities and a major sponsor for the event that formed a key fundraising event in the social calendar.

It would be the first major event that Felix and Ebony would attend together since they formally announced their engagement. Ebony caught a late flight in from Abuja where she had been working on the International Trade project for the organisation her mother was setting up. Felix, whose Lagos flight had only arrived a few minutes before hers, picked her up from the airport lobby and they sat in the car together for the drive to his gated waterside house on the creek marina.

"Wow." Her first word as she stared at the beautiful, six-bed, neo-Georgian style modern house set on three levels, with a boat moored at the marina. She'd thought his Lagos mansion impressive, but for a holiday home, this waterside house represented the epitome of understated elegance.

"Did you decorate this house yourself?" she wondered out loud after he'd introduced her to the housekeeper. They sat out on the balcony overlooking the marina.

"I used an interior designer. I just told her what I liked and she did the rest." He shrugged as if it was no big deal.

"She did a very good job. You have a lovely home."

"It is your home, too, now." He took her hand and kissed her palm. "Let me show you to your room so you can freshen up for dinner."

His words filled her with a mix of anxiety and disappointment. Felix was only fulfilling his part by keeping to a condition she'd set out. Since the day she'd agreed to marry him, he hadn't done anything more that kissing her lightly. She should have been happy but somehow, it left her with a longing to be held in his arms and thoroughly kissed.

She followed him up the grand staircase to a landing that had another informal sitting room and three bedrooms with en suite facilities leading off the hallway.

"This is your room." He opened one of the bedroom doors. "And mine is just over there." He pointed to the door across the hall. "I'll leave you to freshen up." And he walked off.

The room turned out large and tastefully decorated, with cream walls and cool, pastel furnishings. Her luggage had already been unpacked, her clothes hung. They dined together that evening. With Ebony barely able to keep her eyes open afterwards due to fatigue, Felix escorted her to her room and gave her a brief kiss just outside her door.

The next day after breakfast, they visited several of the charities Felix was the patron. First, they checked out the local hospital to open a new maternity wing which the Essien foundation had built. The press photographers were there and Ebony felt uneasy having the flash bulbs going off in her face. But she kept her smile up. Sensing her discomfort, Felix pulled her closer, whispering into her ear, "keep smiling. It'll soon be over." She was glad when they finally left the hospital.

At the orphanage, no media followed them, no cameras. Ebony felt so touched by the children. She played with them, and one particular child tugged at her heart. A little girl, about two years old. Cradling the toddler in her arms, she remembered Felix's unwavering insistence that he didn't want any children. A wave of sadness hit her.

She watched Felix playing a game of football with the children. He looked so relaxed with them. So confident. Surely, he would make a great parent. When he noticed her look of melancholy, he stopped and watched her with an odd expression of his face, one she couldn't decipher.

Later, dressed in jeans and t-shirt, they had visited the local market. Ebony loved the colour, smell, and vibrancy of the environment, the different stalls displaying varied wares, from fresh food produce to beautiful, hand-made jewellery and colourful print fabrics. The market men and women gesticulated and called out to them to buy their wares as they strode past.

She stopped at a stall displaying different items made from coral beads. Curious, she picked a string of waist beads and asked the market seller woman what they were for.

"They are for young maidens. It makes them irresistible to their betrothed and helps with fertility," the woman replied with enthusiasm.

"Oh," Ebony said, heat travelling up her face in embarrassment. Not that she believed in the superstition, anyway. She glanced at Felix but his face remained blank.

"This one will work well for you. With it, your betrothed will be unable to resist you on your wedding night. Here, I'll wrap it up for you," the woman encouraged.

Ebony shook her head vehemently. "No, thanks." She walked away from the stall. What would be the point in kidding herself? Felix was never going to look at her that way.

They walked back to the car.

147

"I forgot something back there," he said when she got into the car. "I won't be long."

Ebony sat in the car and checked her phone messages. One came from the wedding planner, getting back to her about the change of flowers for the reception venue. Ebony sent her a reply. Felix got back soon after that and they returned to his house.

For the governor's ball, she dressed in a sleeveless, coral print, silk maxi dress. A stylist had come in earlier to arrange her hair in a fashionable up do. She carried on finishing her make-up when a knock came on the bedroom door.

Felix walked in. He looked amazing in a black velvet tuxedo, black satin waistcoat, white shirt, and black tie. Her breath caught in her throat and her heart rate increased tenfold. Under his intense scrutiny, her skin mottled with heat and goose bumps. She stood mesmerised, unable to take her eyes away from him.

"You take my breath away, *ima-mmi*."

He kissed her gently, reverently. She melted on the spot. Stepping back, he held up a medium-sized box.

"I've got something for you." He opened the case. Inside sat the most beautiful piece of jewellery made of diamond and yellow topaz stones set in gold necklace and matching earrings.

She gasped. "They are beautiful. You shouldn't have.... Thank you."

"You are beautiful and you deserve beautiful things. When I saw them, they reminded me of your eyes. I want you to wear these tonight. Let me help you put them on."

He opened the clasp of the necklace and turned her so she faced the mirror again. He put the necklace against her skin, closing the clasp at the back of her neck.

"Gosh. I don't know what to say. I feel guilty as I don't have a gift for you."

"You agreed to marry me. That's all the gift I need. I have to confess I have another gift for you." He took out a paper bag from his pocket. "I know it doesn't have the same

148

value of the necklace or earrings, but I found myself drawn
to it as much as I hope you were."

She took the bag and opened it. It contained the
stringed, coral waist beads she'd seen earlier in the local
market. Warm sensation swirled in her belly, and her heart
leapt with joy. He cared enough to have gone back to buy it
for her.

"It's the best gift ever," she said happily. When she saw
his raised eyebrow, she laughed. "Seriously, you don't know
what this means to me." She gave him a brief hug. "Thank
you. I think we better go before I start smearing my
mascara all over you." She sniffed.

Laughing, he took her hand and escorted her downstairs
to the car.

At the ball, Felix proved very attentive, never leaving
her alone for too long. The event was filled with socialites.
She'd forgotten how these nights could get. As a teenager,
she had attended a few similar events when her father was
alive. His work meant that he got invited to such
happenings frequently, and on occasion, she'd had the
opportunity to attend them. They were filled with Nigeria's
political elite and high rollers from the business world. And
of course, there were always glamorous women showcasing
the latest fashion styles and outfits. Suddenly, she
understood why Felix had bought her the jewellery. They
certainly didn't look out of place in the glitz and glamour of
the ball.

Felix seemed to know a few of the ladies at the event by
name. Warily, she wondered at his relationship with them.
He had just handed her a glass of champagne when a tall,
slim woman dressed in a black dress that clung to her body
and left little to the imagination stepped up to him.

"Felix, darling. I was hoping to see you here tonight. It's
been a long time." The woman moved closer to him
provocatively and kissed him on the lips.

"Hi, Helen." He stepped back, immediately putting
some space between his body and the woman's. "I'd like

you to meet my fiancée, Ebony." He put his hand on Ebony's waist in a proprietary gesture.

Helen looked her up and down before turning back to Felix, putting her hands on his chest.

"Nice to meet you, Helen," Ebony said, but she didn't extend her hand. She wanted no contact with the woman who already got on her nerves.

"I did hear a rumour about your engagement but couldn't believe it. You know we shouldn't always believe what we read in the press, right?" She winked at him. "I never thought I'd see the day any woman would snare you. Well, I hope she has what it takes to keep you satisfied."

Ebony's spine stiffened in anger. She would have taken a step forward if Felix hadn't been holding her close. For the first time in her life, she wanted to scratch out the eyes of a fellow woman.

"We are perfectly happy. Thanks for your concern, Helen," Felix replied, his tone nonchalant.

This made Ebony angrier. How could he be so calm when the other woman had practically insulted her?

"Oh, well. If you ever need me, you have my number. Call me." With that, Helen sashayed away.

Ebony moved away from Felix, walking out onto one of the balconies. He followed her.

"What's wrong?" he asked with a tone of irritation.

She rounded on him. "I can't believe you stood there and let that woman talk to me like that."

"I can't believe you fell for her jibe. She was just trying to rile you. I thought you were stronger than that."

"Oh, so now it's my fault. Well, thank you very much." She turned her back to him. How dare he tell her she ought to be stronger? Of course, she was stronger. She would have punched the daylights out of the nasty woman, too.

"Look, she is the daughter of one of our bank's biggest clients. I have to keep her sweet. She's harmless."

She turned round again to face him. "I wonder what else you have to do to keep her sweet," she retorted with disdain.

Felix's eyes narrowed into slits. A muscle ticked on his temple. "What do you mean by that?" He grabbed her arm.

Ebony glared at him. She tried to pull back her arm but he didn't let go.

"So your business is more important than I am," she spat out angrily.

"Oh, come on, Ebony. You're the one who doesn't want any emotional involvement, remember? We're getting married because of the business. Of course, it's important." His voice thrummed low and dangerous.

He had a point. *She* didn't want a relationship. That's what she'd told him. He wasn't marrying her to love and cherish her. It would be purely a business deal to secure his position at Apex Private Bank. She needed to remember it and get used to it. So why did she feel so fragile, so disappointed that she didn't mean more to him?

"Fine. I'd like to go home now. I'm tired." She knew she was sulking but didn't care. The last thing she wanted was to go back into that ballroom and watch all those women he'd probably made love with. One thing he wasn't going to do with her.

He looked at her in silence for a while.

"Fine. We'll bid our farewells."

After saying goodbye to the host and hostess, they left the ball. In the car, they sat in silence for the short journey back to Felix's house.

"I'm tired, so I'll go straight to bed," she said to him when they got inside.

"Good night, Ebony."

Felix walked into the sitting room and she went upstairs. She undressed and ran a bath, filling it with the bath crystals she found in the bathroom. It smelt of blackberries, bergamot, and vanilla orchid.

As she lay back in the relaxing, soothing foams, she pondered upon the day's events. The visit to the orphanage where Felix had seemed at home with the children sat uppermost in her mind. He had played jovially with the kids, kicking about with the new footballs he'd bought them, letting the younger ones take a ride on his back. She hadn't believed it could be the same cool and sophisticated man she knew in Lagos who went to elite bars and drove low-slung, fast cars. To see him playing so freely with the children had been at odds with his wish not to have any.

She rubbed her hand against her tummy and wondered what it would be like to have a child with Felix. If he ever changed his mind, she'd want to be the mother of his children. She wanted him. Now more than ever. She wanted to connect with him. To taste him, feel his essence surround her.

She'd asked for no sex in their marriage. Felix had agreed. So there certainly wouldn't be any kids. Unless she told him she'd changed her mind.

She didn't want other women providing for his needs, giving and receiving pleasure with him. She didn't want women like Helen Douglas thinking they could get their hands on her man. Felix was hers, at least for the next two years. She would ensure it stayed that way.

Feeling emboldened, Ebony got out of the bath and tied on the bathrobe. She put on the waist beads Felix had given her earlier, letting them hang on her hips. This would be as good a time to test their potency. The market woman had claimed they would make her irresistible to her betrothed. Well, that would be Felix, and she needed all the help she could get to seduce him. She took off the bathrobe and put on her short silk robe, instead. Taking a few deep breaths to shore up her courage, she walked out of her room and knocked on Felix's bedroom door.

When he didn't open the door immediately, her boldness fled her body. She turned to return to her room. The door opened. Felix wore only a bath towel low around his waist and water droplets on his body. Nothing else. At the sight of his broad shoulders and rippling flat stomach muscles, her heart started pounding erratically, spreading heat around her veins.

He stared at her with curiosity.

"Can I come in?" she asked, feeling uncertain.

"Sure." He stepped back and opened the door wider, letting her in.

Walking into the room, she took a deep breath and inhaled the zesty scent of his tea tree shower gel. She noticed his massive bed and her already fast pulse went off on another sprint.

"I wanted to say sorry for earlier. I shouldn't have lost my temper. I just didn't like seeing Miss what's-her-name all over you. It won't happen again." She stood in the middle of the room and tried to keep her eyes on his rugged face and not on his beckoning, taut chest muscles.

"No. I should be the one apologising. She was out of order and I shouldn't have let it happen. Forgive me."

"That's good." She smiled and her courage raised another notch. "We were both wrong and we have both apologised, so matter closed, right?"

"Right."

"So, are we still friends?"

"Of course we're still friends." He smiled with his usual charm.

"Good, because I have a favour to ask."

"Ask away."

"I want you to kiss me." She took a step towards him.

"Sorry, kiss you?" he asked, but his eyes twinkled with awakened interest.

"Yes. Passionately, no holds barred." She took another step in his direction.

Now his onyx eyes burned with desire.

"*Ima-mmi*, if I kiss you tonight, I won't stop at just kissing you."

His voice beckoned low and husky, sending heat to pool in her core.

"That's what I'm hoping for because I don't want you to stop." She took another step towards him. Now, she stood close enough to feel his breath feather her face.

"Are you sure about this? You don't have to do this."

"I want to. I want you. All of you." She undid the belt of her robe and let it fall on the floor. She had nothing on except the string of coral waist beads sitting on her hips.

Felix groaned and fell on his knees, kissing and licking her belly button just above the line of the beads while he ran his fingers along the coral. The friction against her body sent more lava pooling between her thighs.

He stood up, pulled her into his arms, and kissed her passionately, thoroughly, just as she'd yearned for weeks. She melted into him, savouring his taste and smell as his hands roamed her quivering body, leaving a trail of heat in its path.

CHAPTER ELEVEN

"Are you telling me this pregnancy...the child in your womb is mine?"

Felix staggered backwards, his injured leg a dead weight. He had to ask the question, though in his mind, it didn't make sense that the child could be his. A strange feeling of déjà vu surrounded him. Like he'd been in this situation before and it had all come to nought. He stared at the woman sitting on the bed in their luxurious beach hideaway. The reason he'd brought her here seemed suddenly inconsequential and pushed out of his mind. He found himself left instead with a cold knot in his stomach and alarm bells going off in his head.

Ebony nodded as he watched her closely, her liquid gold eyes flashing with resolve, her chin set in defiance. "This baby is yours...mine...ours."

They had created a child together? He was going to be a father?

Her words should have cheered him. His heart ached for it to be true. Yet, bile rose in his throat in censure.

"Why should I believe you, Ebony? Why should I accept your word?"

"Because I'm your wife," she retorted, furious.

Sarcastic laughter erupted from him, slicing through the air. "Yet, in the past few days, you've lied and hidden things from me, for your own purposes. And I'm supposed to trust your word now. I don't think so."

"I may not have told you the whole story but I've had no ulterior motive except taking care of your needs. I was simply waiting for the right time to tell you about my pregnancy. It may be hard for you to comprehend but finding out has been a shock to me, too. Especially in light of everything else going on. I didn't plan this." Ebony jabbed her clenched fist into her open palm.

You mean, unlike all the other women who've plotted to acquire a piece of me?

Felix bit back the retort stuck in his throat. He wanted to accept her words at face value. To trust that she was telling him the truth. However, the old feelings of mistrust and betrayal that had eaten away at him for most of his adult life were deeply entrenched. He couldn't simply shake them off. Mostly, he hated that bits of his memory were missing so he couldn't confirm for himself if her story about the night of the governor's ball could be true.

"So what's your plan now?" he asked coolly, though the last thing he felt was cool.

"I have no plans per se. But let's be clear about one thing. No matter your opinion, I'm keeping my baby," she said, her hands covering her stomach in a protective manner.

A sickening feeling coiled in his stomach. What was he doing? Did she think he'd do anything to hurt a child, even if it wasn't his?

"Of course you're keeping it," he snapped back. "What do you take me for? If the child is mine, then he or she is an Essien and will be brought up as one. It's my responsibility to make sure my child is protected and provided for."

"So now it's your child? How convenient. I thought it wasn't yours a minute ago," she rebuffed. "Anyway, what makes you think I'd want to hang around and bring up my child with a pig-headed man like you?"

Rage coursed through his veins. This woman certainly pushed his buttons today.

"Since you've been quite vocal about your intentions, let me be clear about mine. No Essien child has ever been brought up outside our family. I'm not about to change a family tradition. The Essiens take care of their own. You are now an Essien, and so is the child in your womb. Unless you wish to tell me otherwise."

He waited for her to speak. Her mouth opened but no words came out, her face in shock presumably caused by his words. He smiled with derision and continued. "Good. Now get dressed. We are going back to the city."

The silent air in the car on the drive back to the city felt frozen. Ebony got lost in her thoughts and so it seemed Felix, too. Her emotions were all over the place.

Guilt. Fear. Desperation. Anger. Determination. All warred for supremacy in her torn mind.

When Felix had first found out about the pregnancy, his expression had filled her with guilt at her deception for not telling him sooner, for letting him find out by chance. Then he'd walked out of the hut and she'd been scared she'd lost him. That he wouldn't be coming back for her.

However, whilst he'd been out, she'd tapped into her inner strength and her resolve not to give up the child regardless of the outcome. Until he'd turned up and implied the child wasn't his. She'd been infuriated. How could he think she'd be trying to pass off someone else child as his? She wasn't that kind of person. Yes, she'd hidden things from him purely to preserve and make the most of their budding relationship. But she wasn't cruel or manipulative. She didn't even know how to be those things.

Seeing the disbelief in Felix's eyes when she'd told him about their night in Calabar had made her desperate. Right then, she'd frantically wanted him to remember it, too, to believe her words. His distrust of her worried her. How could they possibly move forward if he didn't trust her?

Yet, the biggest shock had been hearing him say, *"The Essiens take care of their own. You are now an Essien, and so is the child in your womb."*

Whilst his words had brought some relief, it had also left her with more questions. Did he now believe the child to be his? Or was he simply stating that, because they were married, the child would be brought up as an Essien though he didn't believe he was the biological father?

She didn't know whether to laugh or cry. She hadn't cried back at the hut. She wasn't about to start now.

The car drove through the wrought iron electric gates, down the drive, and stopped under the portico. Felix stepped out and held the door for her. She noted his courteousness and thanked him. When they got indoors, he turned to her, his expression unreadable.

"I have a few phone calls to make. I'll see you later." He turned and walked towards his office.

"Felix, I...." She trailed away, not sure exactly what she wished to say. She didn't want him to walk away. She couldn't help the feeling this spelled the beginning of the end for their marriage.

He stopped and turned back to face her, his expression back to being cool and unruffled. There lingered no trace of his earlier anger or shock.

"Did you want to say something, Ebony?" He glanced impatiently at his watch.

Overwhelmed by a sudden need to cry, she shook her head and choked out the word, "No," before running up the stairs into the bedroom.

She had been strong all day even when Felix was denying their child. Yet, all it had taken for her to break down had been for him to look with irritation at this watch. She felt so small, so insignificant. She had gone from being a much-cherished wife to an object not to be tolerated. All in the space of a few hours. How did it go wrong? It hurt her more than anything Felix had done before. The pain of his abandonment on their wedding night returned, cracking her fragile heart.

In the bedroom, she sat on the bed as her body racked with sobs, and ended up coiled in a foetal position as she held her shaking midriff with crossed arms. Her phone rang and she ignored it. When it started to ring a second time, she picked it up, swiping her blurry eyes with the back of her hand so she could see the caller ID. Faith. She pressed the call answer button.

"Hi." She went for a cheery tone but failed miserably as Faith noticed right away.

"Hi. What's happened? You sound awful," Faith replied, concerned.

Ebony bit back another sob and coughed to clear her throat. "Nothing. I'm okay."

"You're not okay.... It's the baby. You've told Felix. I'll kill that man if he's upset you. What did he do?"

Ebony smiled forlornly. Her Amazon warrior princess friend was about to kick some male butt. Shame it had to be Felix's.

"I'm okay. It's just been a stressful morning. That's all....Yes, Felix's found out about the baby and he's not overjoyed. But he's doing the right thing, I think."

"Which is what, exactly?" Faith's question came back quick fire, indicating her growing annoyance.

"He said he'll take care of the baby and me. Although he doesn't think the child is his." Ebony choked again.

"What an idiot. Of course it's his. Who does he think it belongs to, for goodness' sake?"

"He thinks it's Dele's. He thinks I've slept with Dele. Can you imagine?" Ebony still couldn't believe it herself.

Faith's laughter sounded acerbic. "Men. They have no clue. You told him you wouldn't touch Dele with a barge pole, right?"

Ebony frowned as her friend's words prickled her conscience. "Maybe not that strongly, but something to that effect. To be fair to him, at least he is not kicking me out yet. That's something."

"That's nothing. You are his wife. He should believe you when you tell him you are carrying his child."

"He should. But remember, he can't recall anything before a few days ago. It can't be easy for him just accepting he has a child on the way when he can't remember making the child in the first place." Ebony defended Felix. He wasn't being nasty, just distrustful. From his history, she understood his unwillingness to take her word for it. It still hurt, regardless.

"Yes, but still. Do you want me to talk to him?" Faith asked.

"No." Ebony spoke firmly. The last thing she wanted was another person getting involved directly in her problems. "I'm sure with time, he will come around."

"I hope so. The last thing you need right now is to be stressed out. Try and get some rest and call me if you need me. You know I'll be there, no problem."

"Sure thing. Thanks a lot, girl. You are always a great help."

The bedroom door opened and the click of Felix's cane against the floor alerted of his presence. Ebony stiffened, keeping her face averted from him. She didn't want him to see her blotchy face or that she'd been crying.

"Bye," Faith said on the other end, to which she replied and switched off the phone.

Still refusing to look at Felix, she got off the bed and walked towards the bathroom. Her body registered his presence, regardless.

"I called the doctor."

His voice came out low and gravelly. It rumbled through her, stopping her in her tracks and she struggled not to turn, not to look at his face. She could feel his body heat, smell his aftershave. She folded her arms under her chest to quell her quivering body.

"Why?" She aimed for nonchalant and hoped she hit it. But her voice sounded strained.

"You are pregnant. You need to be checked out to make sure you and the baby are okay."

What I need is for you to hold me and tell me you believe me—that the child is yours. What I need is for you to love me.

Her thoughts screamed in her head but she kept them to herself and stiffened her stance instead. She wouldn't break down in front of him. She had dealt with more devastating incidents. She would deal with this one, too.

"Fine. I'll freshen up." She walked into the bathroom.

"I'll send him up when he gets here." His words before she closed the door.

Felix watched as his wife shut the bathroom door. He should go to her, take her in his arms and tell her everything would be all right. He also wanted to shake her in frustration and wring the truth out of her. She had been crying. He'd known as soon as he walked into the room and saw the way she sat on the bed. The way her head hung forward as she spoke into her mobile phone. It gnawed at him that he could be the cause of her distress.

God help him.

What was he supposed to do? Why did things have to be so complicated? A day ago, he'd been having the best time of his life. Suddenly, everything seemed to be falling apart. Nearly insane with frustration, he balled his hands, needing to pound out his fury on a punching bag. He needed his memory back. He needed to know if Ebony was telling the truth. He had to be sure. Had to protect himself if it turned out all a lie.

Gritting his teeth, he turned and walked out of the room.

Ebony spent the rest of the afternoon upstairs while she waited for the doctor to arrive. She'd had lunch with Felix mostly in silence and had made her escape from the stifling cold atmosphere as soon as she could.

Before Felix's return home, she'd been spending Sunday lunchtime with the senior Essiens or at her mum's house.

Listless, she contemplated calling her mum to tell her about the baby but decided it would be probably better to wait until things were settled between Felix and her.

She spent the day surfing the internet, searching out information on pregnancy and mums-to-be. The pregnancy was still at a too early stage for her to just sit and do nothing. She had to get busy again.

While Felix had been in hospital, her main goal had been to be by his side. Now he'd come home and spent most of his time in his office, she needed to find a new goal. She could always go back to her job. Her mother had kept the position open for her so she could come back anytime she wished.

She called her mother, after all, who said it would be okay for her to resume work whenever she was ready. No time like the present. So she switched the phone off and went to find Felix.

He was in his office, standing by the window overlooking the back garden, and turned when she walked in. For a brief moment, she noticed his face twisted, as if in pain, then he put his mask of aloofness back on before it fully registered it.

"I need to speak to you." She stood in front of his desk as he walked back and sat down. When he didn't invite her to sit on his lap as he'd done the previous two days, she decided to sit on one of the chairs in front of his desk.

"I'm listening," he said when she got seated.

"I want to go back to work," she blurted out quickly.

"Why?"

"Well, when you had the accident, I took time off work to be with you, but now, you are home and well. I can go back to work. The position is still open. I'm still needed."

He shook his head. "No, you can't."

"Just like that? Why the hell not? You're working. Why shouldn't I?" Close to losing her temper, she glared at him.

"From what you told me, that job involved a lot of travelling, spending most of your time in Abuja. You are pregnant, for heaven's sake. You want to traipse all over the country when you should be taking it easy and resting? I won't allow it."

"I am pregnant. Not an invalid. And it is my life, my body. I won't let you dictate what I can or cannot do." She stood up as her body vibrated with her anger.

Felix watched her intensely for a strained moment before scrubbing his head with his hand and heaving a sigh.

"How about this? The doctor will be here soon. Let's see what he says first. If he thinks it's okay for you to go back

162

to work, then it's fine by me," he said in resignation, his face suddenly looking very tired and strained.

She took a step towards him before realising what she was about to do and stopped herself.

"Fine. I'll be in the upstairs lounge."

She turned and walked out, going back upstairs.

The doctor arrived not long afterwards. Felix showed him upstairs and left them together, closing the door as he departed.

The medic gave her another pregnancy test kit which she used, checked her blood pressure, took a blood sample, and asked her several questions. The kit confirmed the positive result she already knew it would.

He told her that once the blood test result got confirmed, they would book her into the hospital for an ultrasound scan. When she complained about her morning sickness and fatigue, he recommended foods to allay the nausea and plenty of rest. He also gave her some multivitamins. She asked about going back to work. He said it shouldn't be a problem as long as she didn't over-exert herself.

Felix came back into the room when the doctor had finished, looking concerned. But the man soon reassured him all was well. He walked the doctor downstairs.

Not wanting Felix to have to climb the stairs again, she went back down when she heard the doctor leave and met Felix in the hallway on his way up.

"We can talk in the office," she said as she walked past him.

He nodded and followed her into the room. She sat and waited for him to sit down.

Ebony didn't wait for a preamble. "The doctor says it's okay to go back to work and Mum says I can start next week."

"That's fine. However, you need to limit the travelling and work from Lagos most of the time."

Felix's prompt response gave her relief. She didn't want her job to add to the list of things breaking up their relationship.

"Suits me fine." She nodded.

"Good," he said curtly.

Ebony hated that their relationship was breaking down to the point they couldn't even talk to each without it being stilted. Where had the man on the beach yesterday gone? The man she had bared her past to. The man who had made love to her as if she was the most important person on the planet to him. That man had gone, replaced instead by an unfeeling chunk of ice glacier.

The Felix of the past few days had been warm, tender, and loving. This cold and aloof Felix reminded her of the man on her wedding night. Would she ever get back the passionate and tender Felix? Her heart ached for what she knew she was going to lose. However, she had one thing to look forward to. Her baby.

"I'll leave you to it," she said calmly and walked out of his office.

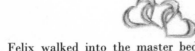

Felix walked into the master bedroom. Late shadows loomed in the room lit only by the dull glow of a little lamp on the nightstand. He inhaled the light, floral scent of his wife—her essence that seemed to fill any space she occupied—before he saw the small, curled up figure on the bed. Her knee almost touched her chin, her arm under her head, her coppery brown hair spread in waves like flames of fire behind her.

She looked so fragile, so vulnerable. His heart seemed to stop for a moment as pain and guilt washed over him. What was he doing? To himself. To her. She was his wife. Surely, they could find a way forward somehow.

He walked over to the settee and sat down as his leg threatened to buckle underneath him. He found himself mentally and physically exhausted. His ankle had been in excruciating pain all day. He'd tried to hide it from Ebony, not wanting her to worry about him. The less concerned she got about him, the better. She had to focus on her health and the baby.

Thankfully, the doctor had said they were both doing fine, although the medic said he would book Ebony in for a prenatal scan as soon as possible. Felix knew he wouldn't be able to relax until that scan carried out successfully. He knew from first-hand experience how tragically things could go wrong. He prayed history wouldn't repeat itself. Although he couldn't shake the feeling it already had.

If he continued to respond to his instincts, then things would work out fine. That's what he hoped, anyway. His instincts had never failed him before. They wouldn't fail now. Yet, something else told him his wife wouldn't lie to him about something this big. That the woman he'd known the past few days had been honest, loyal, and loving. What more did he need as proof?

He took his clothes off and got down to his boxers. He usually slept in the nude but today, he chose to keep the boxers on. As he watched Ebony, his body stirred. He missed her. Missed the fun they'd had at the beach. He needed to keep things simple between them for now, until he resolved the issues between them. His body didn't seem to get the message. It needed her closeness, needed to possess her, to be possessed by her.

He was tempted to sleep in the spare bedroom. What would be the use in running? He'd promised to take care of Ebony. To spend each night with her in his arms. What kind of person would he be if he didn't keep to his words? He owed her that, at least.

In any case, she'd be returning to her job soon. This meant he wouldn't be spending as much time with her as he done previously. He didn't like it one bit. However, he had to live with what she wanted.

He got into bed and lifted her closer, moving her hair out of her face. That's when he noticed the blotches on her face. She had been crying again. In her sleep. His heart skipped a beat. His gut wrenched in agony. This woman meant a lot to him and yet, he turned into the one hurting her. He knew it but was at a loss. What was he going to do?

Gathering Ebony, he held her tightly. In her sleep, she wriggled closer to his body and relaxed into his arms. He caressed her skin. As he listened to the gentle sound of her breathing, slowly, he drifted off to sleep.

CHAPTER TWELVE

Ebony woke up feeling hot. Her eyes flicked open with shock when she realised she lay encased with a warm, hard, muscular body, a firm leg draped across hers.

Felix!

She attempted to wriggle out but he held her close, caressing her arm.

"What are you doing?" she asked, surprised more than anything else. The last thing she'd expected was to wake with him holding her so warmly after what happened yesterday.

"Waking up with you in my arms, like I promised. Good morning, *ima-mmi*."

He kissed her neck and her body responded as usual, melting on the spot. However, the events of the previous day were still uppermost in her mind. She wasn't ready to shove them aside.

"What promise?" She turned around and gazed at him warily.

He had on his lazy, sexy smile that made his cheek dimple and his onyx eyes sparkle like diamonds. Those eyes slowly turned fiery with desire. She felt herself responding, nipples hardening involuntarily.

"I did promise we would spend every night together." He trailed his finger down her face, and she tingled from his touch. "And I promised to take care of you and now the baby, too."

"Even though you don't believe the baby is yours?" The words tumbled out of her mouth even before she could think about them. Could she hope he'd changed his mind?

"It doesn't matter what I believe. The important thing is that you are my wife and I'll do my duty to both of you." His tone sounded indifferent, as if it truly didn't matter.

Instinctively, she stiffened her back. She knew this must be too good to be true. To wake up in Felix's arms as if nothing was wrong. Of course he hadn't changed his mind. She put her hands onto his solid chest and pushed him back.

"I don't care about your duty, you pigheaded fool. I want you to believe me, to trust me."

Even as she said the words, she realised that she might be preaching the words, yet not practising them. Felix had asked her if she trusted him a few days ago and she'd lied. She knew most things about him. Yet, she hadn't been able to trust him fully. How could he trust her when he couldn't even remember anything about her or their marriage? He was the one at a loss. Still.

"I am trying to do the right thing here." He looked wounded and frustrated.

She took a deep breath and let out a sigh. "I know you are. I was thinking last night. Why don't we do a paternity test?"

"No." He sounded vehement, his body tensing as he let go of her.

"Why not? It would put your mind at ease, as well as mine." She looked at him, puzzled. She had thought he'd be keen to have proof of the baby's parentage.

"I still say no." He growled in frustration, scrubbing his head with both hands. When he looked at her again, his gaze didn't flinch. "Ebony, all I need is your word that this child is mine. I'll ask you this only once more. Is the child in your womb mine?"

"Yes!" Her turn to be vigorous. She didn't have to think about it. She knew it to be true and hoped he'd finally believe her.

"Good. That's settled." He moved towards the edge of the bed.

He would accept her words just like that? What brought about the sudden change of heart? He didn't even want a paternity test. Surprised yet again, she tried to decipher his motive and just stared at him, mouth agape, as he sat on the edge of the bed. He'd taken a step of faith in trusting her. It couldn't have been easy for him. She had to return the gesture somehow.

When Felix tried to stand up, she reached out to him. She took his hand and scrambled to her knees on the bed, giving him a hug.

"Thank you for accepting my word, for believing me," she breathed against his firm chest. Shutting her eyes, she inhaled his essence, loving his warm hardness against her body.

Tipping her head back, the intensity of the longing in his eyes speared her.

"You are mine. Never forget that."

Before his words could register in her mind, his lips crushed hers passionately, shutting off all train of thought, focusing her attention solely of the sensations he unleashed within her. Surrendering, she melted against him, her hands clinging onto his solid arms. Their tongues tangled and heat swarmed her.

It wasn't enough. Her thin silk negligee provided minimal barrier between her body and his. The need to be closer to Felix rose. Skin to skin. To feel his possession within and all around her. She glided her hands up his muscular chest and played with his hardened nipples. He groaned before breaking the kiss.

"Please." Was that guttural voice hers?

He leaned his forehead against hers as he tried to catch his breath.

"We can't." His voice came out hoarse and emotional. "I worry about you. You get sick in the mornings. I don't think making love helps. Though the doctor said it would be okay, I'm still concerned about you and the baby. I won't forgive myself if anything happened to either of you."

"I am fine. Our baby is fine." She smiled at him lovingly as her heart ached. This man cared about her and the baby enough to deny himself. When he said things like that, it turned impossible not to love him. "The doctor gave me some vitamins and advice on foods to help with the nausea."

"I know, but I'd rather wait a few more days and make sure everything is fine for myself."

His smile struck her as a strange mix of compassion and yearning. He lifted her from the bed and stood her against him, kissing her again, gently this time.

"But rest assured. It'll be business as usual in the bedroom or anywhere else, for that matter, soon." He straightened and his eyes twinkled with his usual mischief.

Heat washed over her and she lowered her eyes as she smiled coyly. The thought of the two of them in varying positions all over the house twirled excitement low in her belly.

"If you know what's good for you, you better hurry up and make it soonest 'cause I, for one, am intrigued by the anywhere else possibilities," she said shamelessly as she looked up at Felix.

He laughed deeply and she smiled, too.

"You are a gem," he said, running his finger down her cheek. "I have to get out of here before I go back on my word. I have some calls to make this morning but I'll get Bisi to bring breakfast up here for you. So get back to bed."

He kissed her one last time before heading for the bathroom.

Felix sat upstairs in the private lounge of Reams bar, his and Mark's usual nightspot, the first time he'd met up with his brother outside the hospital since his accident. Their kid brother Tony ran the joint, though they'd financed the venture.

They'd been unable to catch up as they'd originally agreed on the phone whilst he was at the beach. His brother had been away for two weeks on business.

Though Mark had volunteered to come over to the house, Felix insisted on coming out instead. Ebony was away in Abuja and the house felt strangely silent and lonely without her.

"So, how are you finally settling into married life?" his brother asked him as he nursed his drink.

Now that he found himself with Mark, reluctance to reveal what bothered him made Felix avoid the subject. They'd been discussing the upcoming meeting with the Apex board of directors to decide his future as Managing Director, the vote being only days away. Considering the weighty problems in his marriage, the possible business coup seemed insignificant in his mind.

"She's not wearing you out already?" His brother's curious gaze turned into mischievous laughter when he saw Felix grimace.

Felix glared at him. "As if."

Unnecessarily irritable, the old Felix would have laughed the joke off. However, he had some serious issues to deal with. He had to get to it and spill.

"She's pregnant," he blurted out.

Mark looked at him sheepishly. "Who's pregnant?" He took a swig of his brandy.

Felix gave him a who-do-you-think glare.

"Oh, Ebony?"

Felix shrugged in response.

"She isn't. How did that happen? Sorry, but you've been in a coma the past two months." Mark looked like he was going to laugh, but held back when Felix looked murderously at him.

"She says it's mine. Conceived on the night of the governor's ball."

"Don't you know? Weren't you there?" Mark spluttered his drink, his eyes sparkling with amusement, which infuriated Felix, but he bit his tongue. Mark didn't know he had amnesia.

"The thing is, I can't remember anything between going to the airport to pick her up the day she arrived in Nigeria and waking up at the hospital bed."

"Are you serious?" Mark's face froze in incredulity.

Felix nodded.

"Shit!" The one word expressed the current state of affairs eloquently. "You can't remember a thing? So there's a possibility the baby is not yours," Mark continued, a frown marring his face.

"She swears it's mine." How he wished it were true. Though he'd accepted her words, deep down within him, doubts still lingered. "She offered to have a paternity test done."

"Yes, we do know how reliable that is—a woman swearing the truth," Mark said with disgust, rolling his eyes upwards. "A paternity test is a good idea. Of course, she could only be saying it as a diversion technique. To get you to think she wants one when she doesn't."

He knew what Mark insinuated, but Ebony was his wife. He had to believe her word even when he didn't have proof. If he couldn't believe her, who could he believe?

Felix turned to his brother and flashed him another withering look. "Watch your mouth. You are referring to my wife."

"Okay. Okay. But you do realise it's only on paper. That's what you agreed to—a paper marriage. Damn. Of course, you don't remember."

Felix froze and the blood drained from his head as his brain tried to assimilate his brother's words.

He had a paper marriage! All he'd shared with Ebony the past few days had been just a temporary act for money and business?

"What are you saying, Mark?" The words came out coldly as his heart became wrapped in ice.

"Your marriage is a business arrangement between you and Ebony. You are paying her a lot of money to stay married to you for two years so you can have time to consolidate your position with the board at Apex PB."

Felix just stared at Mark in disbelief. He'd done that? Married Ebony just to please his board of directors? And paid her to do so? That would explain a few things. Why she'd seemed surprised when he'd mentioned being true

172

husband and wife. Did that explain why they didn't have a wedding night? Maybe. It still didn't explain why he'd left his house that night and had an accident.

So if they'd made a business arrangement, then surely, children wouldn't have been part of the deal. He would have made sure of that, wouldn't he? He wouldn't have wanted to bring children knowingly into a temporary marriage.

He needed to speak to his lawyer. As if reading his mind, Mark cut into his thoughts.

"You need to read the prenuptial agreement. I think there is a clause on any children. And you need to make sure that child is yours, too. Make sure she agrees to a paternity test. Otherwise, this could get very messy."

Things are already messy, Felix thought as he downed his glass in one gulp. The marriage he thought he had didn't exist. All a charade. The only other thought in his mind—he needed to protect his unborn child.

Thinking it was Felix on the line as she headed towards airport exit, Ebony answered the phone with "Hello, gorgeous."

She expected "Hi, beautiful" back from her husband.

Instead she got "Ebony," from a disjointed male voice on the phone.

Stiffening, she pretended she didn't recognise the voice she'd been dreading and almost forgotten. "Who is this?"

"I think you know who it is," the reply came back harsh. "I haven't read or heard anything about your impending divorce. I hope you're not trying to back out of our deal, Mrs. Essien."

Annoyed, she snapped, "You gave me a month and the time is not up yet."

"Don't play smart with me, woman. You only have a few more days to go. What news do you have for me?"

She contemplated telling a lie to get the horrible man who had threatened her husband. It would get him off her

173

case long enough for her to reach home and tell Felix everything. The last two weeks, he'd been the perfect husband despite everything going on between them. They hadn't argued either about the baby or her work. Although she worked from Lagos most of the time, occasionally, like today, she travelled to Abuja. But Felix was always at the airport with the driver to pick her up on her return.

The thought emboldened her. "Look, Mr Whatever-your-name-is, I'm not going to divorce Felix. I love him. In fact, we're having a baby."

"So it's true. You are pregnant."

Her spine prickled that he already knew something only few members of the family knew. A scan a week ago had dated the pregnancy and confirmed the baby to be growing normally. They had celebrated after Felix had confessed his fear. His mother had died due to the complications of an ectopic pregnancy. It had been discovered too late. Her heart had ached for the young boy he'd been then and also for the man who obviously still bore the emotional scars of that loss.

And her love for him had grown ten-fold. Nothing could make her walk away when her husband obviously wanted her and baby.

"I am. Three months and counting," she said with a tight smile.

"You shouldn't have done that, bitch." She couldn't miss the menacing anger in the man's voice. "You're going to pay for crossing me."

The phone line went dead. Her body trembled and she swayed on her feet.

Fingers tapped her shoulders and she jumped around.

Kola caught her, steady hands on her shoulders.

"Sorry, I didn't mean to startle you. Are you okay?" he asked, worry lines on his dark face.

"I'm fine. Is Felix in the car?" she asked, suddenly needing to see him and hold him close. She had missed him these few days. The nights had been lonely and cold without his warm arms around her. She missed his all-too-male

174

scent, his bone-melting laughter, his magical, sizzling touch, and his warm, hard body.

"No. He had a meeting he couldn't cancel." The bodyguard took her carry-on case.

"Oh." Disappointment sagged her shoulders but she held her head high and headed to the car.

Ebony relaxed back into the soft leather of the car seat and closed her eyes for the drive back to Ikoyi. While the nausea had subsided, she was easily exhausted. In no time, the gentle vibrations of the car lulled her into a shallow nap.

As the car pulled through the electric gates, her body hummed with the excitement of seeing the man she loved. Taking her compact out of her bag, she dabbed powder on her face to wipe the shine and loosened her knot, letting her hair fall loose and wavy down her back, the way Felix liked it.

When Kola opened the car door for her, she stepped out, straightening her skirt suit. On second thought, she stopped.

"Kola, please hold this." She handed the silent giant of a man her handbag before taking off her jacket and draping it over her arm. Bag back on arm, she walked to the front door.

Ebony opened it and froze.

The vision in the cool hallway smacked her across the face. She blinked several times, spine stiffened in shock.

Felix, in an embrace with Helen Douglas. Helen Douglas! What was the woman doing in her home? They both turned to look at her as she entered the hallway, Felix's expression one of unaffected disdain. Helen looked like the cat that got the cream.

For a moment, Ebony couldn't breathe. Couldn't think. Couldn't speak. She just watched in horrified dismay as Felix stepped away from Helen to come give her a brief kiss on the cheek.

"Welcome home, darling," he drawled.

Ebony could have sworn there lay a hint of sarcasm the way he said "darling." Come to think of it, that was a new word for him. She looked up sharply and realised he was being sarcastic as his dark brow shot upwards.

"You remember Helen?"

"Hi, Ebony." Helen gave her a cursory glance before turning to Felix. "Thank you for your time today," she purred as she gave Felix a kiss on the lips. "It was absolutely pleasurable. I look forward to our meeting next week."

"Sure. I'll walk you to the car," he said before they both walked out, leaving Ebony standing on the same spot with shock.

Her bag dropping onto the marble floor snapped her out of the stupor. Calmly, she picked it up and walked into Felix's office to wait for him. There had to be a good explanation for what she'd just seen and she wanted to hear it. The image of Helen's arms draped around Felix's body kept swirling in her head, sickening her by the minute. By the time Felix walked back into his office, she had gone from being sick to boiling with rage.

"What was that woman doing in this house?" She got it out even before he reached his desk, her finger pointing in the direction he'd just come from.

Felix shrugged as he walked past her. "In case you've forgotten, I'm working from home at the moment. So my meetings are held here. She did me a favour by coming here."

He didn't sit down. Instead, he walked to the window and stared out onto the terrace.

"So what was she doing all over you? It didn't look to me like just two business associates ending a meeting."

"Are you jealous, Ebony?" He turned to look at her sardonically.

She snorted. "Of course not." She might be feeling slightly envious but wasn't about to admit it.

"I didn't think so, too. Not that you'd care, anyway." He shrugged again, turning back to the window.

His nonchalant attitude wound her up. "What is that supposed to mean? Of course I care. You are my husband."

"You should have thought about that before you decided to swan off to Abuja. It's obvious to me this marriage means less to you than I thought."

How did this suddenly turn out to be her fault? Felix was the one who had been caught in an embrace with Miss sex-on-legs in their home. She'd been in Abuja working.

"Don't be ridiculous. You know very well I couldn't avoid the trip. It was an important meeting."

"More important than me or our baby."

"Felix, you know that's not true." She stood up and walked over to him. "I care about you and this baby." She rubbed her flat belly.

He swivelled around to face her, his expression devoid of any emotions.

"Ebony, you don't have to pretend to me any longer. I know," he said coldly, his eyes like black ice.

She gasped, her heart stopping momentarily. Fear swarmed her. This spelled nothing good. What did he know?

"This marriage is a sham. You're only playing the doting wife because I'm paying you to do it. You sure fooled me." He closed in on her, his fingertip trailing down her cheek, making it tingle. His intense heat surrounding her. "Was it all an act, I wonder?"

His lips descended on hers before she could reply, his tongue pushing past her open lips into the depths of her mouth. She wanted to still her body, to fight her response, but failed miserably. Heat swarmed her, her bones melting into Felix's hard heat. His tongue ravaged her. She clung onto his shoulder to stop herself melting into a pool on the floor.

She returned the kiss fervently. She had missed him these past few days and wanted him, wanted to reconnect with him. He pushed her until the back of her thighs hit his desk.

He lifted his head and looked at her, his eyes smouldering with passion.

177

"I didn't think so," he whispered with need as he kissed her neck, sending more sensation shooting to her belly. "You want me to do this. Yes?"

Unable to speak, she nodded as she tried desperately to draw in breath. All of a sudden, there didn't seem to be enough air in the room.

"And this." He took her nipple into his mouth and sucked and she gasped with pleasure. Even through the fabric of her shirt and bra, she could still feel the wet heat of his tongue swirling around her taut and sensitive nipple.

"Yes."

His hands circled her waist, lifting her onto the desk. Her skirt rode up her thighs as Felix stood between her legs. Rage and passion melded together in her veins as he leaned into her. She couldn't even remember why she was mad at him. The fire in her blood needed slaking.

The hardness of this erection pushed through his trousers at her already wet core. He tugged at her shirt, popping the buttons in the process. They went flying all over the place. He threw the now damaged shirt on the floor and her bra came off next.

Wanting to feel him throb against her palm, she reached for the buckle of his belt. He grabbed her hands, securing them behind her back.

He returned to sucking, licking, and nipping her aching breasts and nipples alternatively as she went mindless with sensation. She wasn't even aware of when he took her skirt off. Only knew when his fingers touched her core, slipping into her, causing her womb to contract in pleasure. Their breaths intermingled as he kissed her again, his tongue mimicking his fingers' actions within her. When her climax came, it caught her unawares, covering her body in feverish heat.

A buzzing phone brought her back down to reality. Felix uttered a low curse, straightened, and picked up the phone on his desk.

"I have to take this. Get dressed."

He picked up her clothes from the floor and tossed them in her direction without even looking at her. The door slammed behind her departing husband, leaving her to wonder what the hell just happened.

CHAPTER THIRTEEN

Felix kicked out even harder as he swam the length of the swimming pool recessed farther back, next to the pool house in the substantial land surrounding his property. He now understood why he'd bought this house when he'd had to escape from Ebony earlier.

Damn it.

That phone call had saved him. He'd been so close to taking her right there and then on his desk when she'd screamed his name as she climaxed.

From the moment she'd walked in the front door, he'd known he was in trouble. She looked sexy as sin with her fiery hair cascading down her back, her shirt buttons undone at the top, revealing smooth, silky skin and a hint of black lace, her feet encased in impossibly high heels that extended her already long legs to heaven. His body had responded instantly. He had to stop himself at just kissing her cheeks. If his lips had connected with hers, he would have taken her there against that hallway wall.

Ebony had thought he'd been interested in Helen. Ironic. She obviously had no clue. He'd been with Helen for over an hour and the only woman in his head had been Ebony. Ms. Douglas might use and dress all her physical assets in a provocative way to attract attention, but she didn't hold a candle to his wife. Ebony's subtle, almost retiring, yet sassy elegance had already stolen his attention from the moment he opened his eyes in that hospital suite weeks ago. No other woman had stirred him so overpoweringly before or since then.

This left him feeling very aggravated.

He pushed off against the wall of the pool and turned to do another lap. Swimming proved the only safe workout he could do without the help of someone else. What he needed to do was take out his frustrations with his sparring partner.

More expletives escaped his lips as he got more wound up about his predicament. Who was he kidding? What he wanted to do was strip away all of Ebony's veneer, have her writhing underneath him while he sank into her deep and wet core again and again. To have her scream his name over and over. So that he knew that she wanted him as much as he wanted her. And not because of any arrangement they might have made.

How had he gotten himself so entangled? Where had Ebony learned such good acting skills? A wonder she hadn't made a career out it. For a while, he'd been convinced he had a genuine marriage. That they'd met and it had been an instant attraction. He'd actually thought this was it for him—he'd actually met someone he could live with, someone he could trust.

Until he'd found out she wasn't even trustworthy. She had kept secrets from him; first their marriage arrangement, then the pregnancy. What else could she be hiding? He knew there had to be something else. Only a matter of time before he found out what. Thankfully, he had spoken to Mark and no longer lay in the dark about her.

In less than two years, Ebony will be leaving you.

The thought flashed in his mind and his gut twisted in response. Why did the thought cause his heart to ache with regret? Why did he want to work out so hard that he ended up mindless and without feelings? Why did he want to tear up that damned prenuptial contract and keep Ebony permanently with him, everything else be damned?

All this for a woman who'd be no good for him. A woman he couldn't trust. Who hadn't told him the most important thing about their marriage. She was up to no good and yet, he wanted her. More than he'd ever wanted anything else.

What was wrong with him?

He let out a loud groan and increased his pace in the pool, swimming a few more laps until the wrenching ache in his heart got overtaken by the excruciating ache in his leg and a throbbing headache. He swam to the edge and pulled himself out of the water. As he wrapped the towel around his waist, he toppled over and reached out to the table to break his fall.

She'll find me.... That last thought crossed his mind as blackness surrounded him.

What the hell just happened?

Ebony paced their bedroom floor, still in the torn clothes she'd come upstairs in, getting more and more wound up. How had she gone from raising hell at seeing Helen Douglas in her husband's arms to sprawling near naked on his desk all in the space of a few minutes? Gone from wanting to spit fire to turning into a pool of needful lava? From wanting to slap his face to wanting him inside her?

She'd had to quickly pull her tattered clothes back on after he'd left her still recovering from the encounter in his office. She'd run back upstairs in embarrassment, hoping none of the domestic staff had noticed her state of undress.

Where was her dignity?

Felix had shredded it along with her clothes, with his behaviour, and she'd allowed it, too.

First, he'd invited that woman into their home. Let her touch him. After Ebony had already told him about her behaviour at the Governor's ball. He knew Ebony didn't like Helen. Even if they had to have a meeting in the house, why did he let her touch him? That's the bit she couldn't get over. Any other woman and she probably wouldn't have been so wound up. But Helen Douglas? She'd known Helen wanted to sink her claws into Felix from the first day she'd met her. The woman had been so blatant about it, too. Well, if Helen thought she'd stand aside for her, she had another think coming. Hell would freeze first.

183

She stopped suddenly as another thought occurred to her.

Felix knows about the marriage arrangement.

How did he find out? Did his memory return? Did someone tell him? If so, who? She knew he hadn't told anyone else about his amnesia except her and the doctors. So she wondered who he'd been talking to. She guessed that it didn't matter. What mattered was that Felix thought that her whole behaviour since he woke from the coma had been an act. That she'd faked it all for money. If only she could pretend. If only what she felt for him wasn't real. She loved the obstinate man with all her heart and had tried to show him that every day. How dare he think she was just interested in money?

Nausea swept over her and she ran to the bathroom, making it there just in time. After throwing up, she stripped off the rest of her clothes and had a quick shower, letting the warm jets massage her back and soothe her. When she stepped out, she felt slightly better.

As she got dressed, she decided on what to do. She would find Felix and sort this whole thing out once and for all. She'd grown tired of walking on eggshells, tired of worrying about the next bombshell. She would tell him everything. He had to know the things that happened the past few days were because of him, only him; not his money or the marriage contract. She was going to tell him that she loved him. Surely, he could see that she loved him. That she wanted to be here with him beyond the originally agreed timescales. Forever. She could only hope that he would listen and accept her. Pray that he felt the same way somewhere in his heart.

Downstairs, she gave Bisi special instructions about dinner then strolled over to Felix's office but couldn't find him there and wondered if he went out in the garden. He loved the outdoors, sitting out in the garden at any opportunity. When he wasn't in his usual spot outside, she headed towards the pool house at the bottom end of the expansive garden.

As she rounded the corner of the pool house, she saw a body sprawled on the stone tiles by the pool.

"Felix!"

With her heart nearly leaping out of her mouth and her legs suddenly wobbly, she ran and crouched over him. He looked lifeless, a pool of blood around his head. Telling herself not to panic and with shaking hands, she checked for a pulse and found a weak one on his neck.

"Somebody, help me!" she cried out as she cradled his head on her lap and hoped someone would come quickly. Tears rolled down her face silently.

Before long, she heard running footsteps and Kola came round the corner in a hurry. He crouched down next to her.

"What happened?" he asked, his normally calm voice carrying concern.

"I don't know. I just found him on the floor and I don't know how long he's been like this. He must have slipped or something."

"The cut on his head looks bad. We have to take him to the hospital," Kola said as he lifted Felix from the floor. She nodded and stood up shakily. He turned to her. "Go and get changed. I'll put something on his head to stop the bleeding and get his clothes on. Meet me in the car."

Ebony started to object before she looked down and realised her clothes were covered in Felix's blood. She didn't care about her appearance while her husband lay injured and needed treatment. She just wanted to get him to hospital as quickly as possible. However, Kola had a point. At the moment, *she* looked like the one injured. She needed to change her clothes.

"Okay. I'll meet you at the car and I'll send the driver to help you."

After one look at Felix, who was now lying on the sun lounger still unresponsive, she ran back to the main house all while her heart pounded with fear that this time death had finally come to claim her husband. Bisi came out of the kitchen. Ebony instructed her to send the driver back to the pool house to help Kola. Then she ran upstairs, stripped off the bloodied clothes, and changed as quickly as she could before racing back downstairs.

When she got out the front door, Kola and the driver were moving Felix's unconscious body into the car. They lay him out in the back seat and she got in and put his head on her lap. They had already bound his head in a bandage to stem the bleeding.

As the car sped off, she called the hospital to tell them what had happened and to prepare for their arrival. They told her not to worry, they'd be ready. All the way there, she kept telling herself not to worry, that he'd be fine. That it was probably just a bump in the head that knocked him out. Yet, she couldn't stop her heart beating fast or her body shaking from anxiety.

It seemed the driver could pick up her fear because he drove faster than she'd ever seen him do. Taking all the side roads to avoid the evening traffic, he got them to the hospital within a short time.

When they arrived, the stretcher trolley waited with the medics outside and they whisked Felix away to an emergency room. Kola stayed with her as the receptionist gave her some forms to fill out, which she did. Afterwards, she sat in the lobby, waiting and praying fretfully.

Felix stirred as muffled voices filtered into his hazy brain. At first, he couldn't make out the words. They were just sounds buzzing in his head. He tried to open his eyes but they felt heavy and his head felt like someone was crushing it with a vise. So he kept his eyes closed and just drifted in and out of his haze as he tried to get a grip on his environment.

He tried to figure out where he could be. The last thing he knew, he was getting out of the swimming pool. Then he'd blacked out and probably fell, the reason why his head felt like someone played a drum kit in there. This meant he must be back in hospital, from the beeping sounds he could hear.

Slowly, the words of the people around him filtered in and became clearer. He could make it out as a man and a woman speaking. The female voice sounded upset and high-strung, the man's tone calmer and relaxed.

"Everything is falling apart," the woman said in a sob.

"It's not as bad as you think. He'll recover." The man's voice felt quieter.

"What if it doesn't? I feel like it's all my fault. Like I pushed him too far."

"It's not your fault. Never think that. He was told to take it easy. He shouldn't have pushed his body too hard. You couldn't have foreseen it."

"But it's my fault things haven't been going well between us. I thought it was getting better, but it all changed again suddenly."

"Look. He is a grown man. He is responsible for his own actions. Stop blaming yourself."

"I'm so worried. What am I going to do?"

"Come here. It'll be okay. You'll see."

Felix body froze as he listened to the conversation, his heart sinking into his stomach as he realised what he listened to. The distressed female voice, he recognised instantly. The male voice sounded oddly familiar but he couldn't place it right away.

There came the rustle of fabric and muffled sound of someone crying. He forced his eyes open though they hurt when the bright light penetrated his lashes. Not even the pounding pain in his head could match the excruciating pain in his heart when his eyes confirmed what his ears had heard.

Ebony, being held closely by the man he had known as his neurosurgeon, Dr. Savage, but who he now realised must also be her ex-fiancé, Dele. They didn't even know he watched them as Ebony stood crying into Dele's shoulder and he stroked her back.

Slowly, a sense of déjà vu descended on him and then the memories came flooding back. He nearly cried out in agony at the pain that racked him.

"Step away from her." His strong words were harsh and deliberate. He didn't care.

Ebony jerked away when they heard him and ran to his side. Dele stood at the foot of the bed, watching.

"Thank God you are awake." She hugged him, tears streaming from her face. He stiffened his body, keeping his eyes trained on the doctor, not wanting to look at his wife whose warmth now surrounded him. He shrugged it off as she straightened, wiping her face with her hands. He had underestimated her. She wasn't just an actress; she was a very good one. He'd nominate her for an Oscar. Even he hadn't seen this coming.

"Leave us," he ground out through gritted teeth, his tone layered with ice, still choosing not to look at her. He had no wish to see her crocodile tears nor did he doubt their effectiveness. After all, he'd fallen for her wily charm before.

"What?" From the corner of his eyes, he could see his wife's puzzled frown.

He growled. Trust her to push him. The charm of her obstinacy had worn off. Did she think he'd put up with it now? He turned to her, his anger simmering in his veins.

"I said, leave us. Don't you understand English? Step outside. I need to talk to the doctor alone." He sounded condescending and insufferable but he didn't care. He'd only just begun. She was going to see a whole new side to him.

"Don't talk to her like that," Dele interjected and stepped forward.

Felix turned and glared at the man, his fury written all over his face. The other man raised his hands and stepped back.

"It's okay," Ebony said in resignation. "I'll go and get a drink."

Felix saw the dejected look on her face before she walked out of the room. He should feel something but he didn't. A chunk of ice now rested where his heart used to be.

"How are you feeling?" Dele asked casually as he came closer to him.

How dare the man? If Felix wasn't lying down, he'd have punched Dele's lights out. Felix ignored his question.

"Don't touch me. I want another doctor." He was surprised his voice sounded so calm.

"I'm the only one available at the moment. I'll check you out and you can have someone else later if you still wish to do so."

"Do you have a problem with English, too? Read my lips. Get. Me. Another. Doctor. Now. Or I'll have you and this hospital tied up in a malpractice suit from here to eternity that you'll never have time to practice, let alone touch another man's wife. And another thing, if you love yourself at all, keep away from my wife. If I so much as get a whiff of you anywhere near her, I promise you will wish you never crossed me. Do I make myself clear?"

The other man stared at him for a while, the casual smile he had earlier wiped off his face. When he finally spoke, he sounded worried. He should be.

"You do realise nothing is going on between Ebony and I. I was only trying to calm her down."

Felix growled menacingly and sat up, ready to stand.

Dele raised his hands in surrender. "Fine. Suit yourself. I'll send another doctor to you," he said before turning to walk out the door.

Felix lay back down on the pillows and waited for his wayward wife to return. His heart ached with such sorrow he wanted to rip it out and be done with it. He didn't want a heart anymore. It proved more trouble than it was worth. What he would have to do next would amount to ripping it out, anyway. He didn't have a choice. Not as he'd remembered everything that had happened in the past and the reason they hadn't had a wedding night.

History had indeed repeated itself.

CHAPTER FOURTEEN

Ebony sat outside Felix's hospital suite and bit her lip. She hugged her shaking body. Kola stood next to her, his normally stony expression softened with concern. He had taken one look at her when she'd stepped out of the room and offered her his seat. She had been glad to sit down. Overtaken by a panic attack, she had felt faint at the time.

After taking a few deep breaths, she felt better now, although her head buzzed with the dull beginning of a nasty headache.

She closed her eyes. The image of Felix's icy cold and angry black eyes loomed in front of her, his lips twisted in disgust, the vein on his temple ticking violently. He looked like a man with murder in mind.

God help her. She had blown it big this time. Baring her heart like that in front of Dele had been bad enough. Dele was an old friend. Whilst she'd never have sought him out any other time, it felt good to have his shoulders to lean on just then. It had been only a brief hug but she could understand how Felix would misunderstand it. Especially if he'd heard everything she'd said. How much had he heard? It looked like he'd caught most of the exchange, gauging from his reaction.

In her own defence, she had been distressed at the time. Seeing Felix back in a hospital room again turned out agonising. If it hadn't been for the quiet strength of Kola and the listening ear of Dele, she would have gone mad with worry.

She now had something different to stress about. It seemed Felix had his memory back. This meant he knew everything about her, him, their marriage, and their non-wedding night.

"Oh!" she groaned out, clutching her head.

"Are you all right?" Kola bent over at her strangled cry.

She nodded but still kept her head lowered.

"I'll get you some water," he said before he walked off, leaving her gratefully alone.

The door to Felix's room opened and Dele walked out. He had a frown on his face. She stood, looking at him with worry puckering her face.

"Is he okay?"

"I don't know," came Dele's terse reply.

"What do you mean, you don't know? You're his doctor," she cut in, confused by his attitude.

"Not any more. He's demanding another medic. And I'm not to go anywhere near you, either."

"What?"

"I'm sorry, Ebony, but you have to talk to him yourself. It's more than my job is worth. He's threatened legal action against me and the hospital if I don't keep away. I'll stay if you want me to, but I still have to get someone else to check him out."

With her mouth agape, she shook her head. "No. No. I'll be fine. There's no point making things worse. If he's threatened you, then he means it."

"If you need me, call me," he said before walking rapidly away in a flurry of white coat.

Ebony couldn't believe Felix had turned down someone who was there to help him, when he lay obviously injured. Dele was one of the best neurosurgeons in Lagos, in Nigeria, even. To get someone as good at such short notice would be difficult. Felix must be angrier than she imagined. And surely, that knock on the head must have caused more damage that she thought. This was plain crazy.

Kola came back with a bottle of water and handed it to her. She took a few refreshing sips and savoured the cool, clear liquid on her tongue.

As good a time as any to face the music. Bracing herself for the worst, she pushed open the door and walked back into the suite. Felix lay back, his face looked strained

192

though his eyes were closed. Slow and silent, her footsteps didn't register against the linoleum of the flooring. At the foot of the bed, she stopped, not sure she should get any closer to him.

"I am sorry," she whispered in a soft voice, her heart wrenching. She wasn't sure if he was awake, if he could hear her.

Icy, antipathy-filled black eyes opened up and pierced through her, pinning her to the spot. Her heart sank rapidly and remorseful tears clogged the back of her eyes.

"Sorry about what?"

His words grated, stung her as sharply as a slap.

"About earlier. About Dele. About the things I said. I wasn't thinking clearly. I was going out of my mind with worry that you'd gone into another coma, or worse."

"Spare me the dramatics. I don't care for it. You of all people understand my need for honesty, loyalty, and privacy. I made that very clear from the first time I met you. Yet, you betrayed me at every opportunity."

"I've done no such thing. I...I—" she stammered, aghast that he would accuse her like that. She would never intentionally seek to hurt him.

"And still you deny it. There's no point talking to you. Go home, Ebony."

"Please, Felix. Let's talk about this. It's not what you think. I'm sorry if you think something is going on between Dele and I. He is only here as your surgeon and I was so distraught. It's not an excuse. I'm sorry. It wasn't my intention to be disloyal in any way. If you want me to keep away from Dele, I promise I will."

"Your promises don't mean anything. You once made me a promise and never kept it. Why should I take your word now, Ebony?"

"What promise? I haven't broken any promises," she said defiantly. He couldn't blame her for something she hadn't done.

Felix shook his head, his lips turning down in a sad smile. "I honestly don't even know which is worse. The fact that you betrayed me by breaking a promise, or the fact that you can't remember making the promise to me in the first place. Shows how little you rate our relationship and, worse of all, me. And to think I thought you were the best thing that happened to me. How laughable? You are quickly turning out to be the worst."

The impact of his words hit her like a punch in the face. Flinching, she racked her brain for what she could have done to make him think so lowly of her. Her racing heart and the tears clogging her vision were not helping.

"Felix, please tell me what's wrong. What I've done? Please. Let's sort this out now. Tonight." The tears were free flowing now. She moved closer to hold his hand. He pulled it back.

"I'm tired of talking. The other day, I told you about my parents and what deception and disloyalty did to their marriage. So you know how I feel about secrets and lies. Go home and think about it. When you are ready to confess, I'll listen. Otherwise, leave me be. The driver will take you home. Go."

He did look tired and in pain. Ebony thought about the wisdom of staying on and trashing out whatever could be wrong between them. She knew she wouldn't be able to sleep until things were resolved. This was her marriage, her life. She had a child to think about, too. If there existed a chance that she and Felix could sort out their troubles, she'd take it.

"Before I go, I want you to know, I love you. More than I've ever loved anyone else."

"Oh, Ebony, you are so full of it." He shook his head in angry whips. "You should have thought about that before you opened yourself up to another man a few days before our wedding."

The bottle of water in her hand slipped out, landing on the tiled floor with a thud. Blood drained rapidly from her head. She felt faint and had to grip the rail at the end of the bed to keep standing.

194

"Yes, I saw you. Though you and your lover made no move to hide yourself from view in your mother's back garden. So stop the all-so-innocent look and get out of here. I'm tired of looking at your face. And another thing. About that baby in your womb, I want a paternity test."

The look of revulsion on his face told her she had to get out of there immediately. Letting go of the bed rail, she staggered out of the room past Kola who she ignored when he called out her name. She kept walking, not acknowledging anyone else until she got outside in the warm night. She kept walking, past the car and driver who looked at her strangely. Out of the hospital premises, onto the road.

She didn't know where she was going but she kept walking, not noticing anything else around her.

He knew. He'd seen. Stupid, stupid woman. What were you thinking? What are you going to do?

The words swirled around in her head, twisting her mind, confusing her. She didn't know how long she walked for or where she could be. At some point, she must have stumbled because she looked up at the bright city lights, the face of Kola looming over her before everything went black.

Felix sat on the settee in their bedroom and watched as Ebony's chest rose and fell silently while she slept, angry at her idiocy for putting their child at risk. What was she thinking by walking into the night like some kind of crazy woman?

As soon as Kola had come into his hospital room and told him Ebony had walked out without waiting for anyone to take her home, he'd told his security chief to find her. Luckily, Kola had seen her outside the hospital and followed her until she had passed out cold on the street.

When the replacement doctor had finally turned up, he had requested an immediate discharge. The medic had protested, saying he should stay overnight, at least, but he'd refused. He had to get out of there, to make sure Ebony and the baby were okay.

Yes, he wasn't a hundred percent certain the child was his, but even by a one-percent chance, he would take it and hope. He would never let a child come to harm, anyway. And since Ebony didn't seem to be capable of taking care of herself better, he would make damn sure that she was taken care of.

When the car had come for him, he'd reached home to find Ebony asleep in their bed. The housekeeper had changed her after Kola put her on the mattress. She still hadn't woken up. He just sat on the settee and watched her. The doctor had told him to sleep, had given him some pills, but he hadn't taken them. Truth being, he didn't want to sleep. He knew what he'd dream about and didn't want it.

So he sat there instead and thought about what he was going to do next.

If there wasn't a baby involved, he wouldn't even be debating it; he would tell the lying woman to go to hell. He didn't need people like her in his life.

How could she have done what she did after she had offered herself to him the night of the governor's ball? So what if, afterwards, he hadn't been the most attentive lover and had avoided her? Still, they had been engaged, were going to get married, even though only on paper. And it had mattered to him. It had hurt deeply. Still hurt, too.

The feeling she had awoken in him on the first night they made love had been so deep, so passionate, so overwhelming, it had scared him. He'd kept himself busy with travel and work for days afterwards, needing the time to sort his head out. He hadn't known then what he wanted but the time apart had been good for him to think. He had come back to tell Ebony what he wanted, only to find her in another man's arms.

Well, she wasn't going to get the opportunity to do that again to him. As soon as the baby came, they would get a divorce. He'd make sure she never came anywhere near him or his child. He'd do whatever it took to make that happen.

Whatever the cost to him.

Felix sat on the settee, drifting in and out of sleep. When the early light of dawn started filtering through the drawn curtains, he went into the bathroom to shower and dress. He came out, took one last look at Ebony, and went downstairs.

Ebony woke with a start. She looked across at the settee and rubbed her eyes. She'd dreamt that Felix slept there last night. Why would he do that? Memories of yesterday came flooding back into her mind. She groaned and sank back into bed.

Yesterday must rank as one of the worst days of her life. First had been the dreaded phone call, then had been coming home to the vision of Felix in Helen's arms and her humiliation on Felix's desk. Afterwards, the horror of finding Felix sprawled injured by the pool house, then his angry and disgusted outburst, and his final stunning revelation. All in all, that she was still in one piece came as a surprise to her.

She wondered how she'd ended up in her bed when the last thing she remembered was lying out on the street after she'd fallen over. Someone must have followed her. Kola, of course. She recalled seeing his face looming over her last night. He would have brought her home.

A knock came on the door and she pulled the sheets higher up her chest, though she wore her nightie. How did she get that on?

"Come in."

Bisi walked in.

"Aunty, *oga* said I should help you get dressed," the petite woman said when she came in.

"Bisi, how can your boss tell you anything when he is not here?" She smiled at the woman cheerily.

"Aunty, he is here. He is in his office." Bisi nodded, pointing downwards.

197

Panicked, Ebony sat up and slid out of bed, coming round to the housekeeper. "Tell me the truth. Is Felix home? When? How come?"

"Yes. He is home. He came back last night after you were—after you came home, *ma*." She shifted her eyes downwards and Ebony realised she must be alluding to her being carried in last night by Kola.

"How did I get into my nightdress? Did you change me?"

"Yes, *oga* Kola brought you in here and told me to get you changed. I did. I hope you don't mind, aunty."

"It's okay. Thank you, Bisi." She turned around but the woman still stood there, unsure of what to do. "Don't worry, I will get dressed myself. You can go."

"But *oga* Felix said—"

"Don't worry about Felix. If he asks, tell him I sent you out." When Bisi still looked worried, she waved her off. "Go on. I'll be fine."

Bisi left her to it and Ebony went into the shower. When she stepped out of the bathroom, Felix stood in the bedroom, looking furious.

"Woman, can you not obey a simple instruction? I sent Bisi to help you. Why didn't you let her?" he growled at her.

"Because I'm not an invalid, damn it," she replied flippantly, standing her ground.

"You would choose to endanger the life of a child, just to prove a point?"

"I haven't put anybody in danger. All I did was take a shower, which I can do quite safely without cracking my skull open, unlike some people I know." She took a jibe at him. What the hell, he deserved it for his attitude.

"Don't push me. You were found last night sprawled on the street in the middle of the night. What were you thinking, walking around like that? You were endangering yourself and the child."

"And what do you care? As far as you're concerned, I am a liar and a cheat, an adul—" She couldn't bring herself

198

to finish the word. "You don't even think the child is yours. So what do you care? It's my body and I'll do with it as I please." Her body shook with rage.

He grabbed her arm tightly and held her still.

"You listen to me. If you think I'll let you harm that child, you've got another think coming. If I have to lock you up in here until he or she is born, I will. Don't dare me."

He let her go and she staggered backward. Without looking back, he walked out of the room, leaving her shaking, half-covered in her towel.

Things were worse than she thought. Strange, but even below his angry outburst, she could still see love masked behind it. She could still see the man she loved. Her marriage might be worth saving; it had to be. What was the alternative? She didn't even want to think about it. If she were going to save her marriage, she would need all the help she could get. And she knew just where to get it.

CHAPTER FIFTEEN

Felix sat in the living room when his father walked in. A brown manila envelope lay on the glass centre table. He knew the content but ignored it.

Being so wired all day, he hadn't been able to concentrate on anything for long. He'd abandoned trying to work to mindlessly flick channels on the wall-mounted flat screen TV, instead. Since their heated exchange this morning, he hadn't seen much of Ebony, either. He'd purposely kept to his office earlier. When he'd heard her go out, he'd gone up to their informal living room area and stayed there for the rest of the afternoon. He heard her come back in about an hour ago and Kola had reported that she'd been to his parents' home.

So it didn't come as much of a surprise to see his father standing in his sitting room now. The surprise was that his father had come himself instead of summoning him to the Essien family home. Not that in his current mood, he would have gone, anyway. Probably why his father came here in person. The old man knew his children well.

"Hello, Dad. This is a surprise," Felix said casually, standing up from the sofa.

"Is it?" His old man apparently saw straight through him by the way he stared at his son. "I need to talk to you."

His father walked to the armchair and sat down. Felix ignored his words and carried on as if he didn't know why the other man wanted to talk. He walked over to the bar area.

"Can I get you a drink?" he asked.

"Not now." His father waved him off. "Come and sit down. I'm not staying long."

He came back and sat on the sofa. "Dad, I know what you're going to say—"

"No, you don't know. First, I've got something to show you."

Chief produced a brown envelope similar to the one on the table. Felix's heart stopped. His father pulled out glossy photographs.

Anguish ripped through Felix's chest as he recognised the images. He closed his eyes and tipped his head onto his hands.

"When did you get them?" he asked.

"A courier delivered them this morning with a note," his father replied. "I presume you got the same because I see the same type of envelope on your table."

Felix lifted his head and stared blankly at the brown parcel. Even with the images covered, they loomed vivid and in Technicolor on his mind. Disgust and rage roiled through him. He jumped to his feet and paced the floor.

"Yes, I got them this morning too."

"Has your wife seen them?"

"No. I can't let her see them."

As much as he was angry with Ebony at the moment, when he found out someone was deliberately trying to hurt his wife, it brought out his protective instincts.

"Does that mean you're going to give in to the blackmail?"

"No way. Kola is already working on a plan. Hell will freeze over first before I resign my position at APB because of blackmail."

"You have less than a week to sort it out before the board meeting," his father said. "I suspect Petersen has a hand in this but we need proof before we can confront him."

"I will bring you the proof, Dad." If whoever was behind this wanted to play dirty, they'd soon learn the Essiens could beat them at it.

"Good. This brings me to the next point. Are these pictures real?"

Felix exhaled. "Yes. I was there when it happened. I walked in on the two of them but they didn't see me. However, I hadn't realised the snake was videoing the whole thing. I would have punched the lights out of him." He still wanted to do so.

"According to the note, they were having an affair while you were in hospital."

"Kola vehemently refutes that claim. He insists Ebony never had the opportunity to meet up with Dr. Savage outside the hospital." He pointed towards the manila file. "Those photos were taken at her mother's house before we got married." He desperately wanted to believe his wife hadn't cheated on him afterwards.

"Then I want to talk to you about your mother and me," his father said.

"What?" Felix hadn't been expecting that and wasn't sure he wanted to hear it, either. "Why now?"

"Because I don't want you to make the mistakes I did. I don't want you to lose your chance at being happy."

This was a first for him. He had a good relationship with his father. They were not best of friends, but he had a healthy respect for the old man and the way he had kept the family—his sons—together despite troubles that hit them. He knew his father cared about him and his brothers even if the man didn't say it.

But his father's relationship with his mother had never been discussed openly. So this came as a huge surprise.

"Look, Dad. You don't have to do this." He scrubbed his face with resignation.

"I have to." His father shifted in his seat and continued. "Our marriage was arranged by our parents, who wanted to consolidate their business arrangement by joining the families. At the time, I was young, carefree, and resented the loss of my freedom in marriage. I didn't care that your mother found herself in the same predicament. I was dating someone else before we married and carried on seeing the other woman even after the wedding. Once you were born, your mother and I got closer, but there was still the other

203

woman. I guess I didn't want to get rid of her. I wanted to eat my cake and have it. Then she got pregnant and everything changed." His father let out a sad sigh.

"Your mother found out about the affair and pregnancy. She wasn't happy but told me to bring the woman into the house. The child was mine and should grow up as a brother or sister to you. I told her it wasn't a good idea. This upset her very much. She started withdrawing and fell into a depression. Nothing I could do about it. That's when she decided we should have another child, that maybe if she did, I would be happier with her. I told her I was already happy with her. I had come to realise she meant so much to me. She said if I cared that much, I would give her another child. We tried and eventually, she became pregnant. But there were complications and she died on the operating table."

His father paused, his eyes clouding over with sadness. Felix just stared at him, his body numb of any emotions. He already knew some of what his father told him.

"The point I'm trying to make is that I didn't realise how much your mother meant to me until it was too late. Despite the way I callously hurt her, she forgave me and my affair and was willing to welcome another woman and child into her home without malice. I wish I could go back and change things but I can't. What I did was bring up you and your brothers together the way your mother wanted. I am glad now seeing the way you, Mark, and Tony have turned out. It is your mother's legacy."

His father leaned forward, staring straight at him. "You were able to forgive me despite what I did to you and your mother. I know whatever the problems in your marriage, no matter how it started, you can still forgive each other and fix it. Don't wake up one day and realise you've lost the most important person to you."

"Dad—" Felix said brusquely as he sat up in his chair.

His father stayed him with a wave. "I've finished what I came to say. Now for the other thing. I brought a DVD for you. Tony converted a lot of the old camcorder recordings into DVD a few years ago. This one, you have to watch. It will help you put things into perspective."

His father handed him a flat case and stood up. Felix looked at the DVD uncertainly.

"I'll see myself out," his father said and walked out.

Felix stared at the case in his hand. *What the hell*. He might as well find out what it contained. So he walked over to the DVD player and slid it in, then turned on the TV. The flat screen flickered and the picture started showing.

The camera zoomed closer to the image of a little boy no older than three or four years old. Felix recognised himself when he's been that young and smiled wanly.

"Felix, guess who we've come to see today?" the adult behind the camera said. His father's voice.

"The baby," little Felix replied as he moved closer to the camera.

The lens panned across a living room to a baby basket and zoomed in closer. Inside the cot slept the cutest little baby girl he'd ever seen, all dressed in pink.

"Well done, Felix. Come and say hello to the baby." This time, the camera panned back to little Felix who was being led by his mother to the cot. He reached into the cot and touched the baby's face so gently. His hand moved down and took her little fist in his and held it.

"Aahh, that's so lovely," the adults in the room cooed.

"Felix, do you know her name?" another adult out of camera shot asked but he didn't know which one.

Little Felix shook his head as he still held onto the baby.

"Her name is Ebony," the adult enunciated.

"Ebony." Little Felix said the word tentatively.

"Yes, Ebony."

The camera moved again as another little boy about the same age as little Felix came into the room.

"Felix, why don't you go outside and play football with Chidi?" his father, behind the camera, asked.

"Daddy, I want to stay with Ebony."

"But Ebony needs to feed. You can come back later and carry her. Would you like that?"

"Yes," little Felix replied, and let go of the baby's hand. Then he ran out with Chidi.

The camera cut to other scenes. They were pretty much the same. Little Felix holding the baby. Little Felix pushing the pram. Then it moved on to other scenes of Ebony as a toddler and playing with a slightly older Felix. There was one of them in a park. From the looks of it, it could have been Hampstead Heath. His family had a home just off the Heath and they had spent a few summers there when he was a child. There were the children, Felix, Chidi, and Ebony—he and Chidi must have been around ten years old from the images, and Ebony would have been no more than five. It must have been some kind of picnic because the adults were seated on blankets on the grass with baskets of food and drinks.

The kids ran around playing football. At one point, Chidi tripped Ebony and she fell down. Felix ran to her, picking her up.

"Did you hurt yourself?" he asked, holding her and she shook her head.

"It's okay, Mum." He turned when the adults were about to get up. "I'll take care of her." Then turned back to Ebony and gave her a hug, reaffirming his words. "I'll take care of you," he said this time to Ebony before turning to Chidi who held the football. "Chidi, you have to play nicely with your sister. You shouldn't be so rough. She is smaller than you."

"Ooooh," said Chidi, laughing at both of them. He ran of chanting. "Felix loves Ebony. Felix loves Ebony."

Felix paused the DVD at that point as silent tears started streaming down his face, blocking his vision. He didn't need the chanting of little Chidi to tell him what he already knew. It screamed evident from his actions on the screen. He loved his wife. Had loved her since she was a little girl and hadn't even known it for so long. How was that possible?

206

Ebony walked into the sitting room tentatively. She knew Felix's dad had been to see him earlier in the evening. But she hadn't seen Felix afterwards and it had grown quite late. She hadn't bothered going to dinner and she knew he hadn't, either, because she'd asked the housekeeper. She was worried because it seemed he hadn't moved from the living room since his father left.

The room seemed dark. The only light came from the flickering TV screen, frozen upon the picture of a young boy holding a little girl. Love and tenderness shone in the boy's eyes. The girl seemed familiar.

Wait a minute. That's me. Who's the boy, and how did that DVD get here, anyway?

She saw Felix's silhouette on the sofa. His head lay bent forward, held by both hands resting on his knees. She walked closer.

"Felix?" She knelt in front of him and put her hands against his on his skull. He lifted his head. She saw tears in his eyes, tears down his face. Her heart stopped momentarily, wrenching with pain.

"I'm sorry. Forgive me, please."

They both said the words simultaneously. Tears welled in her eyes and fell on her cheeks.

He lifted her up and sat her on his knees, giving her a tight hug and placed his head on her chest. She felt the tension gradually leave his body. He rocked her slowly back and forth. Eventually, he lifted his head.

"You hurt me, hurt me." His words were strained, like he found it difficult saying them.

"I realise that and I'm sorry. I don't want to lose you." She held onto him, her tears still streaming down her face.

He used his hand to wipe her tears. "We've both hurt each other. It hurt more because I thought I'd lost you. I'm sorry for lashing out. Can I ask you a favour, though?"

"What is it? Name it," she replied quickly, not even thinking about the implications of her words. She just wanted her man back.

He smiled ruefully. "Maybe you shouldn't be too quick to reply. You may not like what I have in mind." His black eyes pierced hers. Gone was the anguish; just uncertainty remained.

"I trust you to want the right thing for us. Whatever you ask for will be the right thing for our relationship and our marriage. You will never do anything to hurt me or our baby. I see that now and I trust you fully."

He looked at her for a while as if taking in her words. "You don't know how glad it makes me feel to hear you say that. If we are to fully trust each other, then there can be no secrets between us," he said. "I want to know the truth about any situation no matter how bad. I know you may think you are protecting me by hiding the truth, but it hurts more to know you keep things from me than to know the things you kept from me."

"I know I sometimes bottle things up rather than say them. I'll work on changing that. From now on, no more secrets between us." She looked at him, confirming her sincerity with her eyes. His sober yet tender black eyes reflected her emotions.

"I want you to tell me what happened the night I saw you with Dele."

She stiffened and bit her lip worriedly. "Are you sure?"

He kissed her, shutting off her panic and replacing it with passion. When he lifted his head, she wished he hadn't stopped.

"Tell me. Please."

His voice came as a gravelly whisper and goose bumps skittered over her skin. She let out a deep breath before speaking staring blankly at the TV screen as she replayed the events in her head.

"After our night together, you stopped taking my calls. I panicked. I thought you didn't want me and had changed your mind about the wedding. I was going out of my mind with worry. Then Dele showed up at my mum's. He'd heard about our impending wedding and had come to wish me the best. He wished it could be him and I getting married but

208

understood I had to move on. I guess for a brief moment, I wanted to get back what I'd had with him. After all, I had known him for over ten years. He might not be perfect, but at least I knew him."

She turned to look at Felix. "You, on the other hand, I had thought were perfect but I knew nothing about you. I asked myself, why take the risk with you? So when he kissed and touched me, I allowed it. I wanted to find out if I could recapture what we had. As it happened, it wasn't the same. I didn't feel the spark that I get when you kissed me. There and then, I wondered when I had stopped loving Dele and started loving you. Was it the first day we met? Or the first day we kissed? Or the first day we made love? I guess it probably involved all of those times."

Ebony stopped, expecting to see anger in Felix's eyes, but there was none, just tenderness and sadness. She leaned into his chest, letting his hard warmth soothe her.

"Before you carry on, I have a question for you. Please be honest. I won't be mad. I promise. Did he penetrate you that night?"

She jerked in his arms but he didn't let her go. "God, no. I stopped him before we got that far."

The rush of warm air from his exhaled a relieved breath fanned her face. "Thank God for that. I'm sorry if my question upset you but I had to ask to get it off my chest. Please carry on."

He tightened his arms around her. She inhaled and continued.

"I swore that if we got married, I would show you just how much you meant to me. On our wedding day, I was so happy when I arrived at the venue to find you standing there waiting for me. You hadn't changed your mind. I would now have two years to convince you that we were meant to be together permanently. Well, until our wedding night, when you refused to touch me and walked out, instead."

Felix shook his head, his eyes clouding over. "After the night of the governor's ball, I grew unnerved. I was developing these feelings for you that were so overwhelming and I was slowly losing control. The only way I knew to deal with it was to get some space. It gave me time to think. It also gave me time to miss you."

He scrubbed his head with his hand. "I realised that what we had must be so important I had to make sure you knew. I'd raced back from a trip to New York to tell you that I loved you. I was going to cancel the prenuptial agreement. I wanted you to know that when I said 'I do' at the wedding ceremony, it would be the truth and for keeps. Until I saw you with Dele.... I thought you must still be in love with him and probably wanted to get back together with him. I waited for you to tell me but you didn't. On our wedding night, when you told me you loved me, I got so angry. If you loved me, you wouldn't keep secrets, wouldn't have been with a man you knew I didn't want anywhere near you. I got so angry and just drove out into the night. I never saw the truck coming."

She shivered as she remembered that night. "I thought my life to be over when I turned up at the hospital and saw your broken body hooked up to all those life-saving equipment. I know I probably wouldn't have gone on if you hadn't survived."

He squeezed her body tight again. "Don't say that. We are both here. We've been given another chance. Another chance at life and love. I, for one, want to grab that chance with both hands. Our first child in on the way—a child conceived in love, even if we didn't know it at the time."

She pulled back slightly, putting one hand against her belly. "Does that mean you think it's your child?"

"Of course I know it's my child. We both made him, in love and in beauty. You already had my heart before that night, but after seeing you in those waist beads, you certainly won my body forever." He growled in appreciation as his eyes turned a fiery onyx with desire.

Joy flooded her heart and tingles spread over her body at his words.

"Does that mean you'd like a re-enactment of that night sometime soon?"

"Yes, indeed. But not right now. Right now, I want to show you how much you mean to me by savouring all of you right here."

"Before that, I have something else to tell you." She'd debated how to tell him this but the best way would be just to spill it.

"Tell me." He carried on massaging her neck and shoulders, the expression on his face not changing.

"I've been getting crank calls. Some man, I don't know who he is. He never told me his name. But he knows a lot about you and me." Tears misted her eyes.

Felix pulled her tighter, brushing lips to her forehead. "You don't need to say any more if it upsets you."

"No. I have to. I don't want to keep anything from you." She inhaled a deep breath. "The man threatened to hurt you unless I divorced you and I agreed."

"You did?"

"Yes. I'm sorry." She covered her face as shame washed over her. But he pulled her hands off.

"Look at me."

She did and no anger marred his expression.

"It's okay," he said.

"No, it's not. It was on the day you woke up from coma. Somehow, he tapped into my anger at you for spurning me on our wedding night and used it against me. He gave me one month to get the divorce rolling. At the time, I was so angry at you I wanted to divorce you."

"Do you still want a divorce?" Midnight eyes stared at her with understanding and love.

"No. I want forever with you."

"Then, you'll have it. I want forever with you, too." He leaned forward and retrieved something from the drawer under the centre table. "There's something I need to show you. I wasn't going to but since we're no longer keeping secrets from each other, you need to see it."

She turned around and noticed some photos on the table. Due to the dim lighting, she didn't recognise the people immediately.

A couple cinched in a kissing embrace, the woman's dress sleeves fallen off the shoulders and the man's hand on her buttocks.

She leaned closer and gasped. "Where did you get that?"

"They came in the post today along with a note."

Panicked, she clutched his arms. "You've got to believe me. There's nothing going on between Dele and me. That picture was from my mother's garden before—"

He shut her up with a searing kiss. "I know you're not cheating on me."

"You do?"

"I was there that night and that scene is branded in my mind forever, so I recognised the image as soon as I saw it.

Relieved, she puffed out a breath and hugged him. "Thank you."

"Also, I know about your blackmailer." She opened her mouth to refute. He pressed his thumb against her lips. "Your phone is bugged."

Her eyes widened with shock.

"After my accident, Kola took extra precautions. You have to understand he is ex-military and with the rise of kidnapping incidents, he put a tracker on your phone which also doubles as a listening device. He didn't tell me about it until last night when he played back your phone conversation with the blackmailer at the airport."

"Oh. My. God!"

"I know your privacy has been invaded and I'm sorry. Unfortunately, due to the high profile of what we do, the Essiens are a target so Kola has the license to do anything to keep us safe and secure. I've asked him to remove the listening piece but keep the tracking device on your phone. No recording of your conversations are kept. Only the ones with the blackmailer."

"That's something. Thank you. But do you know who the blackmailer is?"

"I have an idea and they are going to pay for threatening you. Nobody threatens you and gets away with it."

"They?"

"Kola believes there's more than one person involved and I agree with him." His grip on her hip tightened. "But you shouldn't worry about that. Right now, I want to make you scream my name."

She laughed as he laid her backwards on the sofa. "Don't you want to finish watching the DVD?"

He turned, smiling wickedly. "We'll watch that later, together. You do realise that's you and me on the screen. My dad brought the DVD when he came over."

"No way." She turned and looked over his shoulder at the TV screen. "Even then, you were smitten with me." She teased him.

"Oh, so smitten," he replied as he took her clothes off one by one.

He made sweet love to her, slowly and tenderly worshipping her whole body. When they were finally spent and cradling each other on the sofa, a thought occurred to her.

"You know we have to thank our parents for bringing us back together again."

He lifted his head. "How come?"

"You dad and my mum had arranged specially for you to pick me up at the airport. Your father told me this earlier when I went to see him. Apparently, they'd been making plans before the board gave you the ultimatum. They just seized the opportunity."

"Our cunning parents. Well, we have a brilliant thank you present for them."

"Oh, what's that?"

"A grandchild."

"And a fantastic present, too."

"I love you, Ebony. You are my love, my heart, and my life, *ima-mmi*."

He said the words she'd been waiting to hear but knew already in her heart.

"I love you, too, Felix."

And she kissed him again, showing her man how much.

Thank you for reading Keeping Secrets. Carry on reading to find out more about the next book in the Essien Series as the story of the Essien family continues with Mark and Faith.

BLURB – MAKING SCANDAL

Sassy, successful Faith Brown has earned her place in the boardroom through hard work and sheer ambition. Making family is not on her agenda when there are businesses to develop and competitors to outdo. So when a casual affair with smooth and irresistible tycoon Mark Essien leads to an unplanned pregnancy, she's determined not to make the mistakes her mother made by living with a man just for the sake of her child.

For Mark, personal matters have no place in the boardroom. Spotting the perfect opportunity, he ruthlessly launches a takeover bid for Faith's Investment Brokerage firm. Finding out he'll soon be a father, he knows he can't let the indomitable and sexy Faith go through with her plans of single parenthood. All gloves are off. He'll seduce her by any tactic necessary if it means his child doesn't suffer the same stigma he did as a child.

With the media dogging their affairs in the boardroom and the bedroom, they find that making family is harder than making scandal.

MAKING SCANDAL – PROLOGUE

Mark Essien strode down the empty aisle towards the boxing ring. On his left hand side marched Felix, his older brother, Kola Banks, their bodyguard, on the man's other side. His brother's pace, controlled and confident, belied the rush of adrenaline pumping through his veins.

Mark knew. Anyone who saw Felix in his blue-with-white-band boxing attire—boots, shorts, robe and gloves—and understood what lay ahead would be clued in too.

Boxing had never been Mark's thing, but Felix enjoyed it as a sport. Apart from training sessions at the membership-by-invitation-only exclusive private gym they used to keep in shape, he had not participated in a boxing fight since his days at university.

Footsteps echoed off the hard flooring, announcing their arrival with the thud of insistent drumbeats. Musk and citrus from air fresheners scented the cool air, wafting from overhead air-conditioning units. Beyond the reach of the aisle spotlights, the rest of the area lay in darkness, the spaced out exercise equipment resembling misshapen, shadowed aliens.

A touch of unease tightened Mark's shoulders. This would be Felix's first serious match since his car accident and the subsequent six-week coma. Had four months been enough for him to recover?

Foolhardy notion to box today. However, no amount of logic from Mark convinced his brother to not fight. Good or bad, determination ran in Essien blood, a trait they all shared and part of the reason their business ventures rocketed with successes.

However, Felix had a wife, Ebony, and a baby on the way; no harm should come to him. They might not share the same mother, but Felix was his brother; his blood. And Essiens stood side by side, in love *and* in war.

Like right now.

In the ring occupying a chunk of the massive well-kitted gymnasium, his brother's opponent leaned against the ropes, his corner men on either side of him. The referee stood at the centre alongside the owner of the boxing club. No one loitered in the sidelines. Kola had arranged this strictly private affair to set things right for Felix.

A lesson needed to be taught. No man messed with an Essien and got away with it.

Kola parted the ropes and Felix stepped between them. Mark stood at the edge of the ring, his hands in his trouser pockets, projecting outward calm when inside his concern for his brother's wellbeing rose. His stomach churned and his mouth dried out. He eyed the cooler at the base of the square platform which contained plastic bottles of mineral water, but didn't pick any.

Felix gave a cursory nod in acknowledgement at the other man. His opponent pulled his lips back, baring blue gum shield in a nasty sneer. This wasn't meant to be a friendly fight. The stakes were too high, almost a winner takes all.

Felix ignored the man's taunt and rolled his shoulders, hopping around on his corner of the ring to keep his heart rate up.

Mark squinted at the opponent jumping and pacing his half of the ring. Stocky, he packed more weight than Felix, so if his brother got hit, he'd feel it. Felix had religiously watched all those videos of Mohammed Ali fights as a teenager. He hoped his sibling had learned a thing or two about avoiding punches.

"Float like a butterfly, sting like a bee," would come in very handy today.

The referee introduced them—Felix Essien versus Dele Savage—read out the rules, and started the countdown to the first round.

Kola took Felix's robe and stepped out of the ring. "Remember, keep moving. Don't let him hit you."

Felix jabbed the air in quick succession, hopped twice, and turned. Mark caught his gaze, leaned onto the hard base below the last rope and said, "Knock him the fuck out."

His brother nodded, bared the white mouth-guard in a grin, and rotated to face his adversary. At the bell, Dele Savage lived true to his name and ran at his brother like a bull, with a jab. Felix ducked and hit out with a left hook, connecting with his opponent's right side. They circled each other. Another jab came at him. He blocked and threw a cross punch.

Watching his brother fight reminded Mark of the first time he'd ever seen Felix throw a punch. As a kid, Mark had been thin and tall, bookish and a little awkward. His confidence and body had filled out later, in his teenage years.

In his earlier days, he'd lived with his mother who hadn't been married to Chief Essien, their father at the time. He'd known Felix was his older brother by two years, though they lived in different homes yet attended the same primary school.

Felix has always been athletic, at home on the sports field. Mark preferred playing a Gameboy or reading a book than doing anything that required physical exertion.

In those days, Mark couldn't understand why he only saw his brother at school, or why they couldn't hang out more frequently. Neither did he understand why he could only see his father once a month.

The kids in his school picked up on this fact and made fun of him. Mark had hated the taunts and lashed out the only way he could, with his acerbic tongue. One lad hadn't taken his blistering words well and had gone as far as pushing him down in the playground.

Like a super hero, Felix had stepped in and asked the kid to back off. Between the heart hammering in his chest and the loud rush of blood in his ears, Mark could barely open his mouth to tell his brother not to defend him. After all, Bully Bami, as the boy was known by the pupils, was twice the size of most kids in the playground and Felix went on a suicide mission by challenging him.

Still, Mark could only watch on as if the actions unfolding before him were from a television screen. The boy shoved Felix in the chest. Felix responded with a jab that landed midriff and sent Bami careening into the circle of kids and onto his backside.

The incident earned them a trip to the Headmaster's office and an earful from their father. But Felix and Mark's relationship had been cemented on that day. Mark developed an awe-like respect for his older brother. When Felix's mother passed on and Mark's father married his mother, they all lived under the same roof, finally, and Mark and Felix became almost inseparable.

Ding. The sound of the bell drew his attention back to his surroundings. The first round ended. Felix stepped back and lowered his body onto the stool Kola placed in his corner.

The bodyguard bounded into the ring and crouched over Felix, outlining Dele's weaknesses and what Felix needed to do, while Mark pulled himself up behind the ropes and rubbed his brother's shoulders, reinforcing his silent presence with the physical contact. Mark's strength didn't manifest in the technicalities of boxing. But his brother would feel his presence and know that Mark stood behind him, with him, in this and always.

The next round went great and quickly. All of Felix's punches hit their mark and he avoided being hit, except for one glancing blow on his shoulder.

In the third round, he caught the man out with a right upper cut, blood flying in the air. A drop splattered on Felix's forehead. Dele hit the deck. The dull, satisfying thud reminded Mark of sacks of food being offloaded out of containers at Apapa Wharf and chucked into mountainous piles.

The bell rang. Air rushed out of Mark's mouth, the tension knotting his muscles dissipating. Not that he hadn't believed in his brother winning the match. He just didn't like watching Felix get hurt.

Moreover he'd never witnessed Felix lose a fight except to Kola. Then again, they were not in the same class. It would be like comparing limes and oranges—Felix's welterweight to Kola's super middleweight. As a former member of the Nigerian Armed Forces, Kola was a trained fighter, built like a bullet-proof armoured tanker, but with the reflexes of a stealth fighter jet.

Kola jumped over the ropes and parted them for Mark to step through. Lips curled in a full smile, Mark embraced Felix, not caring that his torso was slick with sweat and wet patches now stained Mark's blue, silk shirt. Kola patted Felix's face with a towel.

The referee stepped forward and grabbed Felix's hand, lifting it high above their heads as he declared the winner.

Now, to collect the prize.

When Kola's investigation had pointed all fingers at Ebony's ex-fiancé as the man who had taped his encounter with her and sold it on to the blackmailer, Felix, Kola, and Mark had agreed they needed to get back at Mr. Savage. Kola had wanted to throw the man to the wolves or the *area boys*, the local gang of men Kola had mixed with as a kid, who saw Dele's actions as an affront to one of them.

But Felix hadn't wanted a street brawl.

Neither had Mark. He had learned early in life that he could cause as much harm to a person with his brain as with a fist. In those days, what he lacked in superior athletic skill, he more than made up in academic prowess. He learned to read people and understand what made them tick.

One valuable lesson he acquired—people were willing to pay whatever price for an easier life.

So he started charging to do students' homework and tutoring them. Since he was in a private school, all the kids there were from wealthy families, so pocket money was par for the course. By the time he got to secondary school, he hadn't needed the pocket money from his parents. He had a regular income.

So when it came to punishing Dele, Mark's suggestion had been to strip the man of what made him a man—his wealth. Take away his job, house, and car, and make him destitute. This was Africa, after all. And like it or not, a man's worth was measured mostly by his status and lifestyle. Take them away and he would cease to be relevant in society and become nothing. Nobody.

Felix had chosen the boxing ring, instead—a legal and equally painful option—and had thrown the challenge to Dele in a way he couldn't resist. Enter the boxing ring with Felix or face a malpractice suit. And of course, Dele hadn't known his opponent had been an Olympic standard athlete in his prime. Their family home had a cabinet decorated with Felix's tournament trophies.

To Felix, challenging Mr. Savage to a boxing match was the equivalent of a duel, an arrangement to engage into combat between two individuals to preserve one or the other's honour. Not only had Dele betrayed Ebony's trust, he had insulted Felix, in the process.

And according to his brother, "there's no greater satisfaction than the impact and crunch against flesh and bones when you knock an opponent out and see him sprawled on the floor."

Now the rat rocked on his knees before Mark's brother, his face and lips distended from Felix's punches. Kola slipped a smart phone into Felix's hand, the small white towel now hanging over Felix's shoulders.

"I warned you that if you messed with my wife, I'd make you pay for it. You should've heeded my advice," Felix said, his voice raspy from the aftermath of his fight, his chest heaving as he inhaled short breaths.

"I haven't seen or spoken to your wife since that day in the hospital," Dele mumbled through swollen lips, his head bent, his shoulders slumped.

Felix squatted beside his beaten foe. "I believe you. However, pictures of you and my wife were sent to me and my father with a threat of it being published online if we don't meet specific demands. Do you know anything about that?"

"No. I...I don't."

"We'll see. Kindly unlock your phone for me." He held out the phone so Dele could see it.

"I won't. Why should I?" The man lifted his head and glared with defiance, spitting a wad of bloody saliva at Felix's feet.

Kola stepped forward.

Felix appeared to retain his cool, though. "You might consider changing your mind. Unlike me, Kola here has no qualms about disfiguring this pretty face of yours. No woman would want to look at it ever again."

Dele's eyes widened and he pushed off the floor with his hands and staggered backward. Kola bunched his fists and took another step forward.

"All right. The code is 9-3-2-9."

"Thank you." Felix entered the number to the phone keypad and unlocked the screen. He accessed the media folder and scrolled through until he found what he was looking for.

"Well, well, well. So it *was* you. You recorded your time with Ebony and sold it on to a blackmailer. What kind of man are you?"

Disgust rolled through Mark and bile touched the back of his throat. What kind of bastard set up the woman who had once loved him?

"Tell me the name of the man," Felix ordered in a soft tone.

"No. I can't," Dele replied, shaking his head.

Felix nodded.

Kola threw a jab and Dele fell back into the corner of the ring. He lifted his arms to block and punch back, but Kola didn't let up. Each of his punches connected, the pounding sound against flesh and bones reverberating in the space, mixing in with Dele's grunts.

None of the other men in the gym intervened. Not even Dele's corner men. They stood behind the ropes, watching as Kola delivered his own brand of justice and torture.

"Just say the name and he will stop," Mark's brother added after a moment.

"Petersen," Dele shouted in a pained voice. "Kris Petersen paid me to give him information about you and your wife."

Kola stopped throwing punches and stepped back. Felix nodded and gave the phone to Mark.

He opened the back and removed the micro SD card, then threw the phone on the floor where it shattered into pieces. They would retain the evidence and this way, Dele couldn't cause any more damage with those photos.

Dele's supporters suddenly turned up at his side, pulling him up from his slumped position. He shook them off, the snarl on his cut lips broadcasting his displeasure as well as the angry words he spat out in Yoruba.

"My promise still stands. Keep away from my wife so you can live a long life. I won't be so gentlemanly next time."

Felix stepped off the ring and walked out, with Mark and Kola behind.

Kris Petersen – Nil. The Essiens – One.

The fight had only just begun.

OTHER BOOKS BY LOVE AFRICA PRESS

Healing His Medic by Nana Prah

Queer and Sexy Collection Volume 1

His Defiant Princess by Nana Prah

His Inherited Princess by Empi Baryeh

His Captive Princess by Kiru Taye

CONNECT WITH US

Facebook.com/LoveAfricaPress

Twitter.com/LoveAfricaPress

Instagram.com/LoveAfricaPress

www.loveafricapress.com

LOVE AFRICA
PRESS
African Love Stories